# LOVE
# HIGHLANDS

Lavina took her hand from his, but she had the strange feeling that he released her reluctantly.

She went into the corridor, and once again played the tunes which she loved herself, and which she felt expressed in music what she felt when she was riding, dancing or just looking at the sun.

She knew now that her music spoke to the man she loved, and that the things it told him were vital for them both, and the future.

"You must get well, completely well," she told him in music. "I love you more than I can ever say, except in this music which seems to come down from heaven and not belong to the world."

After a while she thought she would see if he was asleep or awake. She went into the room very quietly and found his eyes closed.

She knelt beside him, praying that he would soon get well, closing her own eyes as she did so. When she opened them she saw him looking at her.

# The Barbara Cartland Pink Collection

Titles in this series

1.  The Cross of Love
2.  Love in the Highlands

# LOVE IN THE HIGHLANDS

# BARBARA CARTLAND

Barbaracartland.com Ltd

# THE BARBARA CARTLAND PINK COLLECTION

Barbara Cartland was the most prolific bestselling author in the history of the world. She was frequently in the Guinness Book of Records for writing more books in a year than any other living author. In fact her most amazing literary feat was when her publishers asked for more Barbara Cartland romances, she doubled her output from 10 books a year to over 20 books a year, when she was 77.

She went on writing continuously at this rate for 20 years and wrote her last book at the age of 97, thus completing 400 books between the ages of 77 and 97.

Her publishers finally could not keep up with this phenomenal output, so at her death she left 160 unpublished manuscripts, something again that no other author has ever achieved.

Now the exciting news is that these 160 original unpublished Barbara Cartland books are ready for publication and they will be published by Barbaracartland.com exclusively on the internet, as the web is the best possible way to reach so many Barbara Cartland readers around the world.

The 160 books will be published monthly and will be

numbered in sequence.

The series is called the Pink Collection as a tribute to Barbara Cartland whose favourite colour was pink and it became very much her trademark over the years.

The Barbara Cartland Pink Collection is published only on the internet. Log on to www.barbaracartland.com to find out how you can purchase the books monthly as they are published, and take out a subscription that will ensure that all subsequent editions are delivered to you by mail order to your home.

# THE LATE DAME BARBARA CARTLAND

Barbara Cartland who sadly died in May 2000 at the age of nearly 99 was the world's most famous romantic novelist who wrote 723 books in her lifetime with worldwide sales of over 1 billion copies and her books were translated into 36 different languages.

As well as romantic novels, she wrote historical biographies, 6 autobiographies, theatrical plays, books of advice on life, love, vitamins and cookery. She also found time to be a political speaker and television and radio personality.

She wrote her first book at the age of 21 and this was called Jigsaw. It became an immediate bestseller and sold 100,000 copies in hardback and was translated into 6 different languages. She wrote continuously throughout her life, writing bestsellers for an astonishing 76 years. Her books have always been immensely popular in the United States, where in 1976 her current books were at numbers 1 & 2 in the B. Dalton bestsellers list, a feat never achieved before or since by any author.

Barbara Cartland became a legend in her own lifetime and will be best remembered for her wonderful romantic novels, so loved by her millions of readers throughout the world.

Her books will always be treasured for their moral message, her pure and innocent heroines, her good looking and dashing heroes and above all her belief that the power of love is more important than anything else in everyone's life.

*"Love is even more beautiful than all the hills and lakes of Scotland."*

*– Barbara Cartland*

# CHAPTER ONE
# 1876

The letter was full of warmth and affection.

*It seems a long time since we've seen you, Cousin Edward. Much too long, my dear wife says, and I agree with her.*

"So do I," the Earl of Ringwood murmured, a smile spreading over his broad, kindly face. "I should like nothing better than to see my family after so long, and Scotland is very beautiful."

When he thought of the splendid highland scenery the walls of his library seemed to crowd in on him, making him long suddenly for wide open spaces.

He loved his magnificent London home, and the life he led there. He enjoyed his place at court, his status as a trusted adviser, almost a friend, to the Queen.

He also enjoyed the fact that his beloved daughter, Lavina, was the belle of the ball wherever she went. Beautiful, fashionable, elegant and superb, she made him burst with pride.

She had already rejected five proposals of marriage, one of them from a Duke. Secretly Lord Ringwood was relieved as, since the death of his beloved wife, four years earlier, Lavina, his only child, was all he had to love.

Their life was here in the centre of glittering society, and they would not change it for the world.

Any yet, something about the letter he was reading, with its hint of heather and rivers, mountains and lakes, brought a wistful look to Lord Ringwood's face.

*Of course I know that Scotland is a long way from London*, wrote his cousin Ian, *and you have your duties in attendance on Her Majesty. But I live in hope that one day you and Lavina, who must be grown up by now, will give us the pleasure of a visit.*

"It's about time we did," Lord Ringwood agreed, taking up his pen to reply.

But in the same moment the door opened and his butler announced,

"The Duke of Bradwell to see you, My Lord."

Lord Ringwood rose to greet his visitor, delighted, for this was his oldest friend.

"Hello, Bertram," he said. "This is an unexpected pleasure."

The Duke was a tall, elderly man with an upright carriage. Despite his white hair he had an air of health and vigour, but now his face was troubled.

"I came to give you an urgent warning," he said without preamble.

"It must be really urgent to bring you here at this hour," the Earl observed genially. "I know you hate getting up so early."

"I do," agreed the Duke, "but there's trouble ahead, and the sooner you know, the sooner you can act. I would have come last night, but I had a dinner party that I could not miss."

"Sit down," the Duke said, "and tell me the worst."

His easy tone showed that he did not believe that things could really be so bad.

2

There was a pause before the Duke began:

"I was at Windsor Castle yesterday evening, in attendance on the Queen. After supper we all moved, as usual, into Her Majesty's private room. I expected to discuss the local news and was prepared to be bored, when a messenger arrived with an urgent letter for her.

"She read it through, then said unexpectedly in a sharp voice, 'Another letter asking me to provide a wife for a Balkan Prince, whose country is being threatened by the Russians.'

'I've said many times that I cannot do any more for the Balkans. I have, as you know only too well, provided many English brides to give them alliances with this country.'"

"True enough," the Earl observed. "Who is it this time?"

"Prince Stanislaus of Kadradtz. It's a small place but significant. Herzegovina on one side, Albania on the other. Now they've got Russia breathing down their necks and they expect the Queen to produce a bride, as she has done many times before."

"Well, it's not for nothing that they call Her Majesty 'the Matchmaker of Europe'," observed the Earl.

He smiled as he spoke, but the Duke said,

"You won't smile, old fellow, when I tell you what the Queen has in mind now. Did you know that her great-grandmother was connected with your family?"

"That? Good heavens that was generations ago. We've certainly never preened ourselves on our 'connection with royalty'."

"Unfortunately for you and Lavina, the Queen is counting on it now."

"Lavina?"

At the mention of his beloved daughter the Earl's smile vanished and alarm came into his eyes.

3

"What are you saying, Bertram? Don't tell me Her Majesty is thinking of marrying Lavina to Prince Stanislaus?"

"She's set on it. There were murmurs of dissent last night. Several of the men there had met the Prince and formed a very poor opinion of him. He's a drunkard, a womaniser, and reputedly violent. But Her Majesty refused to listen. She's made her mind up.

"You know how determined the Queen can be. Once she gives you her order you'll be expected to obey.

"If you defy her you'll lose your position at court, and your life will be made a misery. People have tried to stand out against her before, and have become outcasts in society."

"It's a nightmare," the Earl groaned, dropping his head into his hands. "Whatever can I do? For God's sake, Bertram, tell me how I can save my daughter from being forced to marry this appalling man, and being sent away to a far country, living under the threat of invasion."

"I know, I know!" The Duke replied. "I wouldn't want to send a relation of mine there. I've come here to warn you that you will be summoned to Windsor Castle, so that she can tell you herself."

"Damn it, Bertram, what shall I do?" the Earl demanded.

"I can see only two chances for you. One is to leave the country – although she's quite capable of sending a ship to bring you back, or somehow get your daughter married or engaged, before you get the 'Royal Command'."

"How, in God's name, can I do that?" the Earl asked. "Lavina has already turned down virtually every eligible man in London. We can't go back to them now."

"There's one man who might help you, if he would agree to do so, and that is the Marquis of Elswick. If Lavina is already engaged, even the Queen would not expect her to

4

break off her engagement."

The Earl stared at his friend in astonishment.

"You want Lavina to marry Elswick?" he demanded, aghast. "A hard, cold, unpleasant man, without a shred of human kindness in him?"

"Of course I don't want her to marry him. An engagement will do. It can simply be broken off later, when the Queen has found someone else, or sent the Prince about his business."

"I don't believe my ears," the Earl said. "Old friend, I know you mean this kindly, and I'm grateful for the warning, but you must have windmills in your head even to think of Elswick!

"You know he's always shunned all talk of marriage or engagements, after what happened last time."

"I know his future wife abandoned him at the altar," the Duke agreed, "but that was a long time ago."

"But he has never forgotten it," the Earl said. "He loathes women. His country house is only a mile or so away from mine, and it's common knowledge that he'll hardly have a woman in the place."

"Yet he's still the ideal person to help you," the Duke replied. "As you say, he's a curmudgeon, a harsh, solitary man who cares nothing for society, and very little for the Queen, I sometimes think.

"But that's to our advantage, because it means he won't be afraid to offend her, and might, therefore, do as you ask. And he won't talk a lot of pompous nonsense about Lavina being honoured to marry a Prince. He cares no more for Princes than for Queens."

"You think Elswick will actually agree?"

"It isn't likely," the Duke replied frankly. "But I can't think of anyone else who would be of any help at this moment."

5

"All I want," the Earl said angrily, "is my daughter's happiness. I love her, and she's my only child. How can she be happy if she has to live in that barbaric place, with a man of bad reputation?"

"I know," his friend agreed. "At the same time you have to realise that Her Majesty is now in a very difficult position. For diplomatic reasons she can't give the Prince a blank refusal without a very good cause."

"I need a little time to think of the best way to fight this," the Earl said. "Luckily I have until tomorrow."

"Why do you say that?"

"That's when I'm due at Windsor Castle, so I imagine the Queen will wait until then."

"Don't rely on it. This matter is urgent. She'll probably send a messenger to you today. In fact, you're very lucky that the letter did not reach her at a time when you were on duty. If you'd been there she would have cornered you at once."

"Oh heavens, you're right, Bertram. I must leave at once," said the Earl, walking across the room to ring the bell which was beside the fireplace.

Almost at once the butler appeared.

"You rang, My Lord?"

"Her Ladyship and I have to return to the country immediately," the Earl told him. "Kindly inform her of my wishes, then order the carriage and the fastest horses available to come round in an hour's time."

The butler looked a little bewildered at the sharpness in his master's voice. But he merely said:

"At once, My Lord."

Then he left the room.

"So far, so good," the Duke said. "But it's not enough. You're lucky in that Elswick's country house is only a few miles from your own, so you can go home, and seek him out at the same time.

"Ask him if he will become engaged to your daughter or if there is anyone else more socially important that he knows, who can help. Wait! I know – what about the Duke of Ayelton?"

"She's already refused him," the Earl groaned. "He was very offended. Now he's set his cap at an American heiress."

"You have very little time," the Duke said, "as we all know when Her Majesty wants something done she wants it at once. Or if possible, the day before yesterday!"

He smiled as he made the joke, but the Earl was looking very worried. Going to his desk, he picked up various letters which had not yet been opened and put them into his pocket.

Then he noticed the letter from Scotland that he had been about to answer, when this calamity fell on him, and put that into his pocket as well. He seemed to be moving in a dream.

"Suppose Elswick refuses," he said at last. "There must be someone else I can beg – on my knees if necessary – to save my daughter."

"I can think of nobody," the Duke said bluntly. "You know as well as I do that they all want to kow-tow to Her Majesty. The majority of those who we think are friends will do nothing in a situation like this.

"And it would have to be someone really important, like the Marquis, otherwise Her Majesty would simply insist on breaking off the engagement."

The door opened and the butler said:

"The carriage will be ready in half an hour, My Lord. Lady Lavina has been informed, and is getting ready."

As the butler shut the door behind him, the Duke rose from the sofa and said,

"I wish I could help you more, Arthur. You have always been a good friend to me. But an engagement to Elswick, however unlikely, is the best I can suggest."

"Damn it!" the Earl exclaimed. "My daughter isn't going to be forced into this. She is all I have left now I have lost my wife."

At that moment the door opened and Lady Lavina came in.

She was a tall, very lovely girl, and one whose face contained more than mere beauty. It also had strength and character. Her large blue eyes could glow as much with anger as with warmth, and she was never lost for words in an argument.

Some men would be scared away by the force of her personality. Others would find her intriguing.

The Duke thought she was even prettier than the last time he had seen her.

Now with her long hair shining in the sunshine which was coming through the windows, she lifted up her pretty face to kiss her father before she asked,

"What is happening, Papa? Why this rush to go to the country? You said last night we need not leave for a week or two, and we are due to have dinner with the O'Donnells tonight."

"I know," her Father answered. "But the Duke has brought us bad news, and you had better hear it from him."

Lavina turned to look at the Duke.

"Uncle Bertram, whatever has happened?"

"I came to warn your father that you are in grave danger."

"Me, in danger?" Lavina exclaimed. "Whatever do you mean?"

"The Queen is seeking another royal bride to send to the Balkans," said the Duke, "and she wishes it to be you."

Lavina gave a merry peal of laughter.

"I know that must be a joke," she said. "I'm not royal."

"Her Majesty's great grandmother was connected with this family, and that is royal enough for her."

Lavina gave a cry.

"But everybody has always known about that, and nobody has ever made a fuss about it before."

"Her Majesty never needed to make use of you before," the Duke riposted caustically.

"And she wants me to marry – who?"

"Prince Stanislaus of Kadradtz, a thoroughly unpleasant character, drunken, violent and unprincipled. Also, I believe he does not wash."

Lavina shuddered.

"I could never marry a man who did not wash," she said.

"Of course not," agreed the Duke. "So we have to think of a plan to save you, and the best way is for you to be engaged to someone else. Even the Queen would have to respect that, if your fiancé were sufficiently prominent – and of a decisive character."

Lavina frowned.

"My fiancé? What fiancé?"

"The Marquis of Elswick," explained the Duke. "Your only hope is if he will pretend that you and he are engaged until the Queen has found another bride."

"The Marquis of Elswick!" Lavina echoed, astounded. "Certainly not. Anyone but him."

"I know he has the reputation of being a very disagreeable man," the Duke began.

"And it's well-deserved," Lavina said.

"You have met him, my dear?" her father asked, surprised. "You never told me."

"It wasn't exactly a meeting, Papa. It happened three years ago, when I was visiting the Bracewells. He chanced to call in one evening."

"Now there's a thing!" exclaimed the Duke. "I've never heard of him dropping in like that before."

"I've heard that Lord Bracewell owes him money," the Earl mused.

"Ah, that would account for it," said the Duke wisely. "So, my dear Lavina, you thought Elswick's manners cold and unpleasant."

"I believe that is the general opinion of everyone who meets him," she said stiffly.

"But that needn't stop you accepting his help," the Duke pointed out.

"But why should he want to help me? I've heard about how much he dislikes women. Surely he will hardly want to marry me?"

"There is no question of him marrying you," the Duke replied. "All he has to do is to say he is engaged to you. Then later, when the trouble is over, you will thank the Marquis very much for his kindness, and the two of you will end the engagement by mutual consent."

Lavina pressed her hands to her cheeks.

"Oh Papa, you must save me. I don't want to leave you. Can this idea possibly work?"

"It must," said the Earl grimly. "So we must leave quickly, before a courier arrives here from Her Majesty."

Lavina gave a cry.

"Oh yes, let us go now."

Suddenly she turned to the Duke, and flung her arms about him.

"Thank you for everything, Uncle Bertram."

The Earl also advanced on his friend and shook his hand.

"We are forever in your debt," he said. "Thank you a thousand times for warning me. If Her Majesty asks you where I am, perhaps you should say – "

"Good lord, m'dear fellow," the Duke burst out in alarm, "I'm not going to say a word. Once let her get the idea that I know anything and my life won't be worth living."

Then he gave them both a wink and added,

"Just the same, I'll keep you informed of every Royal move, when I return to Windsor Castle."

"I am more grateful than I can ever say," the Earl repeated.

"So am I," Lavina said.

She put her arms on the Duke's shoulders, and kissed his cheek.

"If you save me I will thank you and love you more than I can ever express in words," she told him.

The Duke smiled at her.

"Your father has been extremely kind to me in the past, and I have always wanted you both to be very happy," he answered. "Anything I can do at any time, I only need your command to go ahead."

"You are wonderful," Lavina said and kissed his cheek again.

Then she ran into the hall and put on the coat which the butler already had in his hands. Then she sped out to the carriage. Her father joined her.

The next moment they were rumbling away on the first part of their journey.

"We've escaped," Lavina breathed. "But only for the moment. Oh Papa, we must escape for good. You must save me!"

The Earl put his arms around his daughter, holding her tightly. His face was very set and determined.

It was a long drive from London to Ringwood Manor in Oxfordshire, and Lavina had much time to think.

What she had told her father about her one meeting with Lord Elswick had been true, but not the whole truth.

Three years ago she had been seventeen, on the verge of making her debut in London society. As she had no mother, Lady Bracewell had agreed to sponsor her, and she had visited the Bracewells at their London home to gain a little polish before the night of her ball.

The Bracewells had given a few impromptu dances to help her "get in the way of things before you become a debutante," as her kindly hostess had said. There were many Bracewell offspring, whose young friends were invited to make up the numbers, and they made a very merry party.

One evening, as they were dancing, the front doorbell had rung, and the butler had admitted Lord Elswick.

Lavina had been struck at once by how romantically handsome and melancholy he looked. Tall, dark, with a lean face, noble brow and fine features, he had seemed the very image of a story-book hero.

She had only a brief glimpse of him, as he had been conducted straight into his host's study, but he had made an indelible impact on her heart.

A few minutes later there was an interval so that the dancers could drink lemonade and catch their breath. Lavina used it to put her head together with the young Lady Helen Bracewell, her dearest friend.

"Isn't he handsome?" Helen giggled.

"I think he looks just like Childe Harold," Lavina breathed.

She knew Helen would understand this as they had sighed together over Lord Byron's world-weary haunted hero. In a poem of five cantos, Childe Harold wandered the world, especially the exotic locations, seeking an escape from boredom and melancholy.

Haunted by tragedy, he took refuge in beauty. The world laid its joys before him, and he greeted them with a faint smile that hinted at suffering bravely borne.

Helen's schoolboy brother had snorted with contempt.

"What a clown the fellow is, drivelling with self-pity!"

The girls had driven him off with loud cries of indignation. Lavina especially had been wrathful. How, she wondered emotionally, could anyone be so unfeeling as to speak of the beautiful, agonised Harold, in such a heartless way?

Harold had haunted her dreams by night and her fevered imaginings by day. She had been quite sure that when she went into society she would find no man who lived up to his romantic presence.

And then the door had opened, and 'Harold' had walked in, pale, dark-eyed, intense, moving loftily above the vulgar crowd.

She was sure that she read suppressed emotion in the brief bow he gave to Lady Bracewell, and secret suffering in the indifference with which he surveyed the dancers.

Ah, she thought, with the passionate fervour of seventeen, such pleasures were not for him. They could not assuage the secret wound that blighted his life.

She was not sure what that secret wound might be, but when Helen whispered that he had been abandoned by his bride on the very day of the wedding, everything became perfect.

The dance resumed. As she turned this way and that Lavina tried to keep her eyes on the door through which he must come when his meeting with Lord Bracewell was over.

She knew what must happen when he emerged. Lady Bracewell would invite him to join the impromptu ball. He would do so, reluctantly. Then he would see her and grow still as heavenly recognition swept over him. They would gaze into each other's eyes, each knowing that the die was cast.

He would forget the heartless female who had abandoned him, and henceforth think only of Lavina.

The thought was so glorious that there was suddenly an extra spring in her step, and she bounced about spinning dizzily. The other young dancers stopped to watch her, while her partner stepped back to let her dance alone.

Oblivious to everything but her own joy she whirled and spun in an ecstasy of delight. For a glorious moment the whole world was hers to relish.

The music slowed, then stopped as she sank into a deep curtsey while the other young people applauded her. When she lifted her head she was looking straight at Lord Elswick.

He was staring at her very hard, but his expression was a blank. With the confidence of extreme youth she interpreted that blank to please herself. Obviously he was stunned by her beauty and grace.

Lady Bracewell was talking to him now, smiling, indicating the young people. Lavina edged a little closer so that he could see her better.

And then he shrugged, turned away, and over his shoulder came floating back the terrible words,

"My dear Jemima, you must forgive me, but I have better things to do than romp with children."

From the mature heights of twenty Lavina could see that, as insults went, it was fairly mild. Since she had not made her debut she was, officially at least, still a child. So it was barely an insult at all, merely a statement of fact.

But at seventeen her sensibilities had been lacerated. Suddenly she became aware of her breathless state, her tousled hair, her flushed cheeks. She had behaved like a hoyden and now she looked like one.

Oh heavens!  Oh, disaster!

Worse still, she heard the sound of a suppressed giggle from behind her.

Like every beauty she already had her enemies, girls of her own age who professed friendship but seethed with envy, and were secretly glad to see her crest lowered.  And now they could laugh at her.

That night she had sobbed into her pillow and sworn that she would never, never forgive Lord Elswick as long as she lived.

Now, sitting in her carriage on the way to ask his help, she supposed she would have to forgive him.  Anything was better than being forced into marriage with Prince Stanislaus.

But she wished it had been anyone but Lord Elswick.

# CHAPTER TWO

The Earl's family had lived in Oxfordshire for five hundred years.

In 1390 King Richard II had made Baron Ringwood a grant of lands and money. The Baron had built a magnificent country house which each generation had improved upon in size and value.

In the Civil War the Ringwoods had been staunchly on the Royalist side, resulting in Charles II elevating the title to an Earldom. Ringwood Place was now an imposing residence with a grand exterior of white stone, and an extensive park where peacocks wandered, uttering their eerie screams.

Lavina had been born there, and she loved the place. Since she had been old enough to remember, the grounds, and the lake where she had learnt to swim, had always seemed like fairyland.

Now the prospect of leaving it, and the country she loved, filled her with dread.

How could her father persuade the Marquis of Elswick to agree to a fake engagement, when it was well known that he loathed women?

It came from the way he had been treated when he was very young. He was, in fact, not quite eighteen, and was attending Oxford when he fell very much in love with a pretty girl whose father had bought a house on his estate.

The girl and the young Viscount, as he was then, had met and fallen in love while they were out riding.

He had loved her madly, and been sure that she loved him equally. He was determined to marry her in the face of all social difficulties, including his parents' opposition.

But he had no money, except what his father allowed him, and if he married her he would be cut off without a penny.

Undeterred, he set the wedding date, certain that his father would relent. In this, he was wrong.

"But it doesn't matter," he told his bride. "What does it matter if we're poor, as long as we love each other."

But she had wanted money and the delights it would bring. On what should have been their wedding day, she had run off with another man, leaving her groom, abandoned and ridiculous, at the altar.

He had never got over it.

"I hate all women!" he had said once. "I trust none of them, and I swear they will never torture me again as I have been tortured now."

He became well-known in the county for hating women, and entertained mostly men at the castle he had inherited when his father died.

He frequently travelled abroad, but never seemed to form any attachments there.

In many ways he was a benefactor to the part of the world where he lived. He helped to improve the county and was a generous friend to a number of people who were in trouble, or too poor to look after themselves.

He was a member of several London clubs, and was popular with the men who frequented them. It was there he met those who waited on the Queen, including Lord Ringwood.

He was thirty-three, yet gave the impression of being older, because of the legends that had swirled around him for more than a decade.

"I really can't believe that he is going to help us," Lavina sighed as they discussed matters during the journey.

"He might, simply because he would disapprove of anyone being forced to marry someone they did not love."

"But would that overcome his dislike of women?" Lavina asked. "On the contrary, it might give him pleasure to refuse his help to a woman, and send her away to be unhappy."

The more she thought about it, the gloomier the prospect became.

At last Ringwood Place came into view. The carriage swung through the main gate for the journey through the grounds. There were the familiar trees that Lavina loved, the great pond, with contented ducks paddling on it. Even in her distraught state the sight of these well-loved signs of home had the effect of calming her.

As soon as they reached the house Lavina sent for the housekeeper and ordered a light lunch that could be served quickly. The sooner they were on their way to Elswick Towers the better.

Then she hurried up to her bedroom where her trunks had already been carried. Jill, her maid and Mrs Banty, her dresser, were already at work, unpacking.

Mrs Banty was a middle-aged woman with an air of imperious authority, whose pride was to be able to locate any of Her Ladyship's garments and suitable accessories at any time, day or night. That ability was to be tested now.

"I'm going to Elswick Towers," Lavina told her, "and I want to look utterly superb."

"The pink," Mrs Banty said without hesitation, pointing to a trunk that, to the casual eye, looked just like the rest. "It is in there."

In moments they had extracted a 'visiting' costume of pink silk, trimmed with four flounces, each surmounted by a band of purple velvet ribbon. The over-skirt was of a heavier, ribbed silk known as faille. This was a lighter shade of pink, trimmed with white lace, with purple velvet ribbon and bows.

Working like the expert she was, Mrs Banty produced the perfect accessories, a tiny parasol of the same pale pink as the overskirt, and a white chip bonnet, trimmed with purple velvet ribbon, and tiny pink rosebuds.

The ensemble was completed by the daintiest pair of black kid walking boots.

As soon as she had finished her lunch Lavina sped upstairs to put on the dress that Mrs Banty and the maid had lightly pressed and brushed out.

Reverently they helped her put it on. When everything was in place Lavina regarded herself in the mirror, wondering if this was all a dream. Surely there was a kind of madness in running away from London at a moment's notice, to throw herself on the mercy of a man who hated women?

But then she took another look at the magnificent creature looking back at her, and she had to admit that she was proud of what she saw. This was no romping child, but a great lady of the highest rank. She looked glorious enough to enchant any man. But could she move the heart of Lord Elswick? Or was he as heartless as the world said?

There was a knock on her door. It was her father.

"Are you ready my dear?"

"Quite ready, Papa," she announced in a firm voice, and walked out with her head up.

Down below, an open carriage was waiting for them, drawn by two white horses. The coachman got onto the box and they drove away, Lavina using her little parasol to protect her face against the brilliant sun.

It was twelve miles to Elswick Towers and the route lay across open country. England in summer was at its most beautiful, and as they bowled along the lanes Lavina vowed again that nothing would make her leave this place, no matter what she had to do.

Even if it meant enduring Lord Elswick.

Suddenly she sat up straight, her attention riveted.

"What is it, my dear?" her father asked.

"Over there, Papa," she said, pointing to a figure on horseback, about a hundred yards away. "Isn't he magnificent?"

"He?"

"The horse."

Horses were Lavina's passion and all her attention was for the animal, which was black and glossy, the most magnificent horse she had ever seen. His skin was like satin, and although he was a huge beast he moved as gracefully as a dancer, soaring easily over hedges and streams, galloping strongly and seemingly without effort.

Only belatedly did she look at the man, whom she realised was riding bareback without saddle, reins or stirrups, holding onto the huge animal's mane and controlling him without effort. He wore only breeches and a shirt that was unbuttoned, showing a broad, muscular chest.

At first she thought he must be a groom, but then something familiar in the set of his dark head made her heart start to beat more strongly.

"Elswick," she whispered.

"Eh – what?" her father demanded. "By George yes! It is Elswick."

The Marquis was in the distance now, getting smaller and smaller, heading in the direction of Elswick Towers which had appeared on the horizon.

As they neared it, Lavina could not help being impressed by the castle which had been restored and added to by the Marquis's father. It was a building of great splendour and magnificence, which cast Ringwood Place into the shade.

In the centre of the main wall was the huge keep, a tower with battlements, at the top of which was a flagpole, telling the world whether or not the Marquis was at home.

The pole was empty now, but as Lavina watched, the flag was hauled right up to the top. Lord Elswick had returned.

As they drove nearer to the castle, crossing the bridge over the stream which ran in front of it, she could not help but be impressed by the flowers which were a brilliant colour at the base of the walls. Also the huge beautifully carved portico over the front door.

The horses came to a standstill in front of it. The footman beside the driver jumped down and rang the bell.

As he did so the Earl said,

"Now, dearest, you stay here. I will speak to the Marquis, then send for you."

"No, Papa, I should come with you," she insisted. "After all, this concerns me."

"Of course it does, but it will be a difficult request to make, and I feel that modesty demands that you should not be present when I ask him to become engaged to you."

For once her gentle father was stubborn, and Lavina had no choice but to agree.

On opening the door, the butler seemed somewhat surprised to see the Earl. However he informed him that he would see if His Lordship was at home.

He moved slowly and loftily down the length of a wide corridor. After a few moments he returned to say that Lord Elswick would receive him.

He then led the Earl down a seemingly endless series of passages until he flung open a door and cried in a loud voice,

"The Earl of Ringwood to see you, M'Lord."

As the Earl entered the room the Marquis, who was sitting down reading a newspaper, put it down.

Rising to his feet he walked towards the Earl.

"This is a surprise!" he exclaimed. "I thought you were in London."

"I was," the Earl said, "but I have come to ask for your help in one of the most difficult and unpleasant situations in which I have ever found myself."

The Marquis had reached home only a few minutes earlier and was still wearing the extremely casual clothes he had worn for his ride. Hearing that he had a visitor, he had attempted some semblance of propriety by throwing on a jacket, but it was an old garment that looked as though it was normally worn around the stables. Which, in fact, was true.

At first glance it gave the Marquis the air of a groom, yet nobody could have sustained that illusion for more than a moment. His height and lofty manner, the haughtiness in his lean face, marked him as the bearer of one of the highest titles in the land.

His dark eyes were vivid and expressive, his mouth was wide and would have been mobile, save for the tense, stern expression that too often settled over it.

Now he spoke politely to Lavina's father.

"I am, of course, at your service. Will you have a drink? I suppose you have had luncheon."

"I had it when I returned home," the Earl said, "after driving from London at an almost incredible speed."

The Marquis raised his eyebrows.

"Good heavens, what can have gone wrong?" he asked. "Surely there has not been an accident at your house or anything like that."

"No, the house is all right and so are the horses, as far as I know," the Earl replied.

"But I have come to you on a very different matter. In fact, to beg your help, and if you cannot help me I think I shall go distracted."

He spoke in such a desperate way that the Marquis stared.

"Let me get you a drink," he repeated. "I'm sure the trouble you're in cannot be as bad as you think it is."

"It is worse," the Earl told him gloomily. "If you can't help me we'll have to leave the country as fast as we can."

"We?"

"My daughter and I. When I think what her fate could be – " he groaned.

"Good Heavens!" the Marquis exclaimed. "What have you been doing and how have you found yourself in such a mess?"

"I'm desperate," said the Earl. "So desperate that I'll do anything you ask, if only you will help me."

"Very well, sit down and let us talk, man to man."

*

In the garden Lavina wandered slowly, looking at the flowers. Then, leaning on the bridge, she gazed down at the water bright in the sunshine moving beneath it.

"I wonder how Papa is getting on," she mused. "He seems to be a terribly long time."

Suddenly she straightened up.

"I should have gone with him,' she thought. "How can the Marquis possibly make a decision like this? What am I doing, meekly waiting out here while two men decide my fate, and exclude me?"

It was also exasperating to have taken so much trouble

over her appearance, and then not to be seen. How was Lord Elswick to know that she was no longer the child he had scorned, if she let herself be banished like a – like a child?

Lavina was not a conceited young woman, but she knew the truth about herself. She knew that she was beautiful, with a touch of magnificence in her looks. Her figure was tall, slender, and superb.

She knew that her luscious dark hair and blazing blue eyes could reduce men to jelly. She had seen it happen too often to have any doubts about that.

When he had last seen her she had worn her hair down in childlike fashion. Now it was up in a stylish coiffure that revealed her long, elegant neck.

She did not want to marry a foreign Prince, but she knew she was fit to be a Princess and she was not averse to letting the Marquis see her.

It might even make him reconsider his dislike of women, she mused, and at that thought a mischievous smile played about her lips.

Not that she was interested in him. The days when she had swooned over a fictional Byronic hero were far behind her. But it would be pleasant to make him regret his callous behaviour, especially if it made him more willing to help her.

She began to walk decidedly towards the house.

As soon as the butler opened the door she said,

"You admitted my father a few minutes ago. "Where is he, please?"

"In the library, miss – er that is – "

"Your Ladyship," Lavina informed him. "I am Lady Lavina Ringwood."

"Your Ladyship, my orders are that they are not to be disturbed."

"That doesn't apply to me," she said firmly, sailing past him. "Where is the library?"

24

"Your Ladyship – " the butler said imploringly.

"The library, if you please."

Perceiving that he was in the presence of a very determined female, the butler yielded and led her down the labyrinth of passages that led to the great room at the back, where ten thousand books had been collected over generations.

Lavina did not wait for him to announce her, but threw open the door herself. Her father turned to look at her in surprise, and the Marquis rose from the chair in which he was sitting.

The library was very large, and it took her a long time to walk across the floor to stand in front of him. During that time she was able to form a strong impression of him.

This was certainly the man she had seen riding with such skill and confidence. She noted that he dressed more like a stable hand than a Marquis, his jacket shabby, his shirt torn open at the throat.

But it made no difference. This man was an aristocrat to his finger tips. He offered no concessions to convention, fashion, or even manners, because he did not need to.

As Lavina walked towards him he did not hold out his hand. He merely stood regarding her with a look in his eyes which told her he was amazed, and none too pleased, to see her.

In fact, she sensed that only courtesy prevented him from ordering her out.

She went to stand directly before him, watching his face for the moment of astounded recognition.

It did not come.

His expression, as he stared at her, was completely blank, save perhaps for irritation.

"I am Lady Lavina Ringwood," she said. "Forgive me for coming in without being invited, but I felt that it was only fair, when my father was asking you for such an incredible favour, for you to know all the facts."

"And you have come here to present me with new facts?" he asked haughtily.

"*I* am the fact, sir. I am the person you are being asked to save, and who would rather die than marry this stranger."

The Marquis stared at her. But he did not speak.

For a moment there was silence while their eyes met. Then she said,

"I am not exaggerating. I would rather die than marry a man who I have never seen – and who, reputedly, does not wash."

The Marquis grimaced.

"I dare say there are worse things in the world than a man who does not wash."

"Not if you're married to him," Lavina said firmly. "Besides, I would have to leave everything I have known and loved since I was born, and be isolated in a country which I have not even visited, with a man who has no use for me except as a weapon against the Russians."

As she finished speaking Lavina could barely repress a sob.

But for a moment neither the Marquis nor the Earl moved or spoke. Both men seemed stunned by her sudden intervention.

"I know we are asking you for a great deal," she persisted, "but I see no other way to escape the Royal Command."

The Marquis regarded her through narrowed eyes.

"Are you sure you've considered this proposal carefully?" he asked.

"What is there to consider? I don't know this man."

"You know he's a royal Prince, ruler of a country, albeit

a small one. These tiny Balkan states are all very grand, and as the Princess you will have all the jewels any woman could desire, a host of ladies in waiting, all addressing you as Your Royal Highness."

Lavina's jaw dropped. She could hardly believe she was hearing such a thing.

"Doesn't the thought of such luxury appeal to you?"

"It most certainly does not," she said furiously.

"Then you're different from most women, who swoon at the sight of jewels," the Marquis snapped with a touch of savagery in his voice.

"I don't care for jewels," she snapped in return. "When I marry it will be for love, and I won't allow myself to be sold off to a stranger, no matter how many jewels he has to give."

"Fine principles for a fine lady," he sneered, "but how long will they last? Wait until they drape you with diamonds – diamond tiara, diamond aigrette, diamond necklace, bracelets, rings, diamond shoe buckles – "

Suddenly he stopped. A strange, wild note had entered his voice and he was breathing hard as though tormented by some violent emotion. He seemed to become aware of his guests staring at him, for he swung away and put both his fists on the desk, leaning on them.

After a moment he straightened up and turned back to face them. He had regained his composure but his face was dreadfully pale.

"Forgive me," he said in a strained voice. "Sometimes I am not quite myself. This is not a good day to come asking me favours – "

"It is the only day I have," Lavina cried. "Only help me and I promise, in fact I swear, that I will not bother you in any way. I will not demand anything from you, except to pretend we are engaged until the danger from the Russians is over. Then we can separate, as undoubtedly you will wish to do, and you never need see me again."

When he did not answer she repeated desperately,

"I swear to you on all I hold sacred I will leave and make no further demands on you, the moment I am safe."

He was looking at her now with a thin, chilly smile playing about his lips.

"Do you know what you are suggesting? We become engaged, stay that way for a while and then – what – ?"

"Why then, we announce that we have decided that we will not suit," she said quickly. "It's easy, engagements get broken all the time and – "

Then she saw his bitter eyes on her, and knew what she had done.

Of course, this man had been jilted at the altar, to the derision of the world. He was the last person who would help her with a false engagement.

She saw defeat staring her in the face, and she began to feel desperate.

If only he would speak. His silence was becoming un-nerving.

At last the Marquis did speak, heavily, as though speech were an effort for him.

"Lady Lavina, I am sorry to hear of your predicament, but I really don't know what I can do. What you suggest is quite impossible. Nobody would believe it. It's common knowledge that I don't live in society, so where could we have met?"

"Surely that is no real problem, sir? It's true that you are seldom seen in society, but you go into it sometimes. Lord and Lady Bracewell, for instance, are friends of ours, and I believe you are acquainted with them."

Now he would ask her how she knew and she would remind him that he had been in the Bracewells' London house three years ago. And he would recognise her.

But he only shrugged.

"I have not seen the Bracewells for some time. We could hardly have met there."

"Not recently, but – "

"If not recently, when? Just how long ago are we supposed to have met? And how did we renew our acquaintance? Or have we both been secretly pining for years?"

His cool, bored tone made Lavina grind her nails into her palm. She fought hard to keep her temper, but it was slipping away from her.

"As a matter of fact we have encountered each other at the Bracewells – "

His brow furrowed.

"Have we? Surely not?"

Only the recollection that she was a lady prevented Lavina from slapping him.

"Please don't waste time trying to remember me, Lord Elswick," she said with spirit. "I assure you I haven't wasted the ghost of a thought on you, and I most certainly haven't been pining for you."

"I'm relieved to hear it, ma'am. Now we can have nothing further to say to each other."

He turned his back on her, walked across the room and stood with his back to his visitors, looking out of the window into the garden.

Everything about him was redolent of finality.

It was over.

Her future was unimaginably horrible.

# CHAPTER THREE

She had thrown away her chance, Lavina realised, if, indeed, there had ever been a chance.

If only she could have contained her temper and not flared up at Lord Elswick. But how could any woman contain her temper with this insufferable man?

She moved towards her father and sat down beside him on the sofa. He put his arm round her and she leant against his shoulder.

"That was very brave of you, my darling." the Earl said in such a low voice that only she could hear.

"I cannot do it, Papa," Lavina replied. "I cannot marry the Prince. But it's no use hoping that this man will help us. We had better go, and try to think of something else."

They rose, and the Earl spoke with dignity.

"I am sorry to have troubled you, sir, and will do so no longer. I must try to find another answer to the problem. I don't know what it can be, but I will never allow my daughter to go to Kadradtz and marry that monster."

The Marquis swung round.

"What did you say?" he asked quietly.

"I said I will never allow – "

"You mentioned Kadradtz."

"Yes. It is Prince Stanislaus of Kadradtz she would have to marry, a man of whom I have heard many vile things."

30

The Marquis nodded.

"All of them true. He is notorious."

"Then you understand my determination to protect my daughter?"

"Only too well," the Marquis agreed. "You are quite right."

Then he began to walk towards them from the far end of the room. He stopped just far away for him to survey them, saying in a harsh voice,

"You have certainly brought me a terrible problem. I don't like telling lies or assuming a false position."

"You have made that very plain," Lavina said coolly, "and I am only sorry that we have imposed on you. We will leave at once."

"Sit down, young woman," the Marquis said harshly. "Allow me to finish speaking. As I say, I object to pretence, but I object even more to this way of bundling a helpless young woman off abroad as though she were no more than a pawn."

He paused a moment before saying,

"I am prepared to enter this false engagement if it is the only way I can help you."

"But – " Lavina stammered, not certain that she had heard correctly, "you just said that you would not help us."

"Never mind what I said then. Listen to what I'm saying now. I am prepared to do as you wish."

For a moment both the Earl and Lavina were silent in astonishment.

Then the Earl said in a voice which sounded strange,

"If you mean that, I can only say 'thank you' from the very depths of my heart."

There were tears in Lavina's eyes. As she spoke, two of them ran down her cheeks.

"Thank you – thank you!" she murmured. "I have been so frightened – you are kindness itself and I am so very, very grateful."

"That's enough of that," the Marquis said brusquely. "I don't want thanks, and I'm not kindness itself. I never do anything that doesn't suit me, as you will soon understand. And please don't bore me with the waterworks. I can't stand weeping and wailing females."

"I do not weep and wail," Lavina flashed. "I was trying to be pleasant to you, to express my gratitude for – "

"Very well, there's no need to say any more," he said impatiently. "Kindly keep your emotions for some time when I am not present."

Lavina gave him a furious glance, but, reading only indifference in his face, bit back her words and seethed in silence.

If anybody had told her that it was possible to be so furiously angry with a man who was doing her a favour, she would not have believed it.

"Lord Ringwood," the Marquis continued, "you may inform Her Majesty that your daughter is engaged to me. I give you leave to say all the right things and contact all the right people, but understand that I want no part of it."

"Of course," the Earl said eagerly. "I'll do everything."

"I suppose there'll have to be a devil of a fuss," said the Marquis, sounding bored. "It can't be helped. You'd better come and stay here for a while."

The grating sound of his voice robbed the invitation of all semblance of generosity, and prompted the Earl to say,

"That's very kind of you, but we don't wish to inconvenience you."

"Inconvenience me?" echoed the Marquis, as though he could not believe his ears. "Of course it inconveniences me. But I've given my word, and when I say I'll do a thing, then I do it properly. Rooms will be prepared for you, and I will expect you tonight."

He turned a hard look on Lavina.

"You will not, under any circumstances, marry Prince Stanislaus, because I will take whatever steps are necessary to thwart him. You have my word on that."

"I – thank you," she stammered. There was something in his look that almost frightened her.

"Do you understand?" he repeated. "I will do anything that is necessary. Anything."

For a moment Lavina was too taken aback to speak, Lord Elswick's manner was so strange. It was as though he were looking through her towards a far horizon, where he could see something that he wanted, and which had nothing to do with her.

To her relief he resumed speaking in a more normal voice.

"We must go about this properly, and be prepared for any eventuality. The Queen will be annoyed, no question about that. She will also, probably, be suspicious."

"Yes, I'm afraid she will," the Earl agreed with a sigh.

"She'll set people to watch us, and report back to her how we behave. If you come and stay here it will look more convincing. Have you heard from her yet?"

He shot this question out suddenly at the Earl.

"She's had no chance to reach me," he replied. "I left London too quickly."

"If she doesn't find you at home in London she will send her messenger to Ringwood Place. She had better not find you there either.

"In fact it's best if a notice appears in *The Times* as soon as possible. We can do that by telegram."

"I've never sent a telegram before," said the Earl, who

was nervous of new-fangled inventions.

"I send them sometimes, or rather, my secretary does it for me. The local newspaper office has a cable facility by which they transmit news to London, so we'll use them."

He sat down at his desk and began to write the announcement. The Earl passed the time by looking around some of the books. He was not an imaginative man, and he had completely missed the currents of emotion and agitation that had swirled between Lavina and the Marquis.

Lord Elswick took advantage of the Earl's absorption to indicate for Lavina to sit beside him so that he could talk to her in a low voice.

"It is as well that you understand me," he said quietly. "In a moment my secretary will arrive, and I will give him the announcement. Once that has been sent off, the die is cast. Do you realise what that means?"

"Of course," Lavina said.

"I'm not sure that you do. It means that I will not be made a fool of. When our engagement is announced it will last until I say otherwise. I and I alone will decide when and how it is terminated. Is that quite clear?"

Lavina did not answer. She was outraged at this manner of talking to her and longed to put this arrogant man in his place. But she did not dare. She needed his help too badly.

After a few moments of silence he looked up and saw her face, full of outrage.

"Be as angry at me as you like," he said coolly. "I care nothing for that, so don't bother to tell me about it. I am not fooling, madam. If you want my help you will do as I say, in every particular. Swear to that now or so help me, I'll turn you out to meet your fate."

"I have no choice," she said in a voice of deep mortification.

"On the contrary, you do have a choice. You can tell me to go to the devil."

"And marry Prince Stanislaus?" she asked bitterly. "I would rather die."

The Marquis shrugged.

"Oh, I don't think so. One says these things, but one doesn't die you know. Life goes on, somehow. Are you going to give me the promise I want, or shall I tear up this announcement?"

"I promise," she said in a low voice.

"Good, then we understand each other. You will find me a most attentive and devoted fiancé, and I expect the same from you. That will be necessary if we are to carry this off."

Without waiting for her to answer he held up the paper on which he had been writing and said,

"There, I think that will do."

He rang a bell and after a moment a young man with an austere manner entered the room.

"Hunsbury, I want you to send a telegram immediately," said the Marquis. "The engagement is announced between Lady Lavina Ringwood, daughter of Lord Ringwood, and Ivan, Marquis of Elswick.

"The bride and her father are currently paying a visit to Lord Elswick's estate in Oxfordshire."

Hunsbury was too well trained to allow his astonishment to appear by more than the very slightest hesitation in his manner. He took the slip of paper the Marquis held out to him, glanced at the words and hurried out of the room.

"Now he'll tell everyone, and it will be in *The Times* tomorrow morning," the Marquis said. "The Queen will read it over her breakfast, and that may save you a deal of trouble."

"It would be a great relief," said the Earl.

"Let's just hope it doesn't occur to Her Majesty to contact you by telegram."

"She hates the things," observed the Earl.

"Good. Go home now, get what you need, bring whatever servants you consider necessary, and arrive back here as quickly as you can."

"Then I shall bring my maid and my dresser," Lavina told him defiantly. She was resolved that this man, who disliked having women in his house, should never be able to say that she had not been honest with him.

"Whatever you please," he replied, sounding uninterested.

"I mention it," she said firmly, "because you are reputed to have no women in the house, even servants."

His head jerked round to look at her suddenly, and his eyes bore a look of cold malevolence that almost made her flinch. Then it was gone.

"You are mistaken, madam," he said distantly. "I have very few women here because it is a bachelor residence, and the house is run by a butler, rather than a housekeeper. But there are several female maids doing the cleaning."

"The menial tasks, in fact?" she said.

She knew she was unwise to be going out of her way to provoke him, but, despite the fact that he was to be her saviour, he annoyed her more than any man she had ever met.

He regarded her, baffled.

"Do not maids dust and clean in your own establishments?" he asked.

"Well, yes, but – "

"Then I am at a loss to understand what point you are making."

"It isn't important," she said, chagrined.

"I am not quite the ogre that legend appears to paint me, and you are welcome to bring any female servants that you wish. Just tell them to stay out of my way.

"Hurry now, so that you can return to your home and leave it quickly. And make sure you tell everyone in your household before you leave, that's the best way to spread news."

There was a touch of bitterness in his voice as he added,

"Servants love nothing better than to gossip about their masters."

"We'll go at once," agreed the Earl.

Lavina took a step forward. Her anger had faded. Now all she could think of was that he was saving her from a terrible fate, and she spoke earnestly.

"Thank you! You have helped my father and saved me. We are both very, very grateful to you."

The Marquis did not look at her as she was speaking.

But as she finished he rang the bell which was at the side of the fireplace. The butler appeared so quickly that he must have been just outside the door, and it was clear, from his face, that he had already heard the news.

"My guests are leaving," said the Marquis, apparently unaware that his butler's eyes were popping. "Show them to their carriage".

"Very good, M'Lord," the butler said, holding open the door.

Lavina held out her hand to the Marquis, but he did not take it. In fact, he put both hands at his sides and bowed from the waist.

Lavina was astonished to realise that he would not touch her.

Then, as if she understood, she dropped her hand and said,

37

"Thank you! Thank you from the bottom of my heart!"

She turned away to her father, and they walked from the room together. She did not look back, and so she did not see Lord Elswick watching her with a strange expression on his face.

Only when they were in the corridor did Lavina realise that the Marquis had not followed them, as courtesy indicated, and as a man would normally do for his fiancée.

So much for being an attentive fiancé, she thought.

Or perhaps this was how he thought attentive fiancés behaved!

The news had spread through the house like wildfire. As they walked through the corridors towards the front door Lavina realised that they were being watched by a hundred eyes.

Servants looked out to catch a glimpse of the woman who had apparently achieved the impossible. If she looked at them they vanished, only to reappear the moment she had passed.

But in the hall they were lining the stairs, frankly staring. And just before she climbed into her carriage she glanced back to see the windows crowded with faces.

As they went down the drive, Lavina turned towards her father and clasped his hand between her own.

"We have won, we have won!" she said.

"I hope so and believe so," the Earl replied. "At the same time, my darling, you may find that strange young man somewhat difficult."

"It does not matter," Lavina answered. "I can put up with him, because I know that in the end I will escape him. After all, the worst I know of him is that he is very rude. And the best I know of him is that he is putting himself out to help me."

"He certainly seems to be exerting himself to do

everything thoroughly," the Earl agreed. "His idea about the telegram was excellent. And after he had refused us so definitely, too."

"Yes, it was strange how he changed his mind so suddenly," Lavina mused. "In fact, I can't help the feeling that he's doing this for his own reasons, and not for us at all."

"Yes, I too received that impression," agreed her father. "But how it could matter to him I can't imagine."

Then, because he had a romantic heart, he added,

"I remember it happened when he turned round. I wonder if he saw you in a better light, realised how beautiful you are, and fell instantly in love with you."

"*Papa!*" she exclaimed scornfully.

"All right, my dear, it was just one of my fancies, you know."

"It's an appalling idea. Rude, arrogant, insufferable, bigoted – "

"If this is how you talk about the man who's doing you such a huge favour, I dread to think what you'd say about an enemy," her father observed mildly.

It flashed through her mind that, in his own way, the Marquis was an enemy, but she did not trouble her father with the thought. He would not have understood.

Instead, she replied,

"That's quite a different thing. He's the last man in the world I'd want to have in love with me. Why, he'd be almost as bad as Prince Stanislaus."

Her father patted her hand.

"If you say so, my dear."

*

As soon as they reached Ringwood Place both Lavina and her father realised that something had happened.

The butler, who admitted them, was in a state of agitation.

"The Queen's messenger called while you were away, My Lord," he said, holding himself very upright, as befitted a man who spoke of the Queen.

"Oh heavens!" Lavina exclaimed. "Already. I thought we would have a little more time."

For a horrible moment she could see all their gains slipping away.

"Never fear, my darling," the Earl said, trying to sound more certain than he felt. "I will be very firm."

"But this man has obviously come to take you to see Her Majesty. How firm can you be when you confront her face to face?"

The Earl, who was wondering that himself, drew himself up.

"I shall say what has to be said," he declared. "They shall not have you. Where is the messenger, Denton?"

"He is not here, My Lord," the butler declared. "He left a letter which he required me to give you as soon as you arrived. And here it is. He says he will return in an hour."

The Earl took the letter and mopped his brow. But as he was about to open it Lavina whisked it out of his hand.

"How unfortunate that we should have missed him," she said. "Please bring us some sherry to the library, Denton."

Taking her father by the arm, Lavina guided him into the library and spoke in a low, hurried voice.

"Papa, we must leave immediately."

"But my dear, how can we? It was different before this letter arrived. Now that I've received it I have to obey its commands."

"But Papa, you have not received it."

"Yes I have. You saw Denton – "

"We haven't seen Denton because we haven't been

home. We have been visiting Elswick Towers, where the Marquis invited us to stay. We did not return here – "

"But my dear, we did."

"No Papa, we didn't."

The Earl blinked in confusion.

"Strange, I could have sworn we just arrived home."

"You're imagining it," Lavina said firmly. "Actually we're still at Elswick Towers."

Faced with his daughter's stronger personality Lord Ringwood yielded and admitted that he was still at Elswick Towers.

"We sent a groom back home to announce that we were remaining there," Lavinia continued, "and our things were to be sent over."

"But Denton would have sent the letter over with our things."

"In the confusion, the letter was lost," Lavina said firmly. "It did not come to light until later this evening. You cannot be accused of ignoring the Queen's command, because you knew nothing about it."

"But suppose the messenger follows us to the Towers?"

"The Marquis can deal with him. He's unpleasant enough to deal with anything. But we must leave quickly. Hurry Papa and give your valet instructions, while I talk to Mrs. Banty."

She sped away and got to work with a will, leaving the Earl to fortify himself with sherry.

First Lavina went to the stables and ordered that another carriage, a closed one this time, should be brought round to the front door, with two fresh horses harnessed.

Then she approached Denton, giving him the delightful smile that made any servant eager to do her bidding.

"Denton, you're such an old friend of the family," she said, "that I want you to be the first to know, that I'm about to announce my engagement to the Marquis of Elswick."

Denton's eyes opened at little wider at this astounding news, but he was too well trained to do more than murmur,

"My felicitations, Your Ladyship."

"Thank you, Denton. Now I need your help. The Marquis has invited Papa and me to stay at his home for a while. So we did not return here, and know nothing about the letter."

Denton looked shocked.

"My Lady! Do you mean that I neglected to pass on the Queen's letter?"

"I realise that it's something you would never do," she said in a coaxing voice.

"A blot on my record," he said, deeply offended. "Which, I may say, has never been blotted before."

"I'm asking a great sacrifice, I know."

"Will the Queen send me to the Tower of London for losing her letter?"

"I won't let her," Lavina promised.

"Well, I may have given it to the under footman to look after. He is notoriously forgetful. Leave matters to me, My Lady."

"Thank you, Denton. And when the messenger returns, kindly tell him that he can find us at the Towers.

"Very good, Your Ladyship."

"You will explain about my engagement – "

"Then it is not a secret?"

"Oh no. You may inform the household, and the Queen's messenger."

She hurried away to her room.

Luckily the visit to the Marquis involved very little

preparation, as they had only just arrived from London, and most of their clothes were still packed. Mrs Banty received her instructions with a brief nod, and assured Her Ladyship that everything would be attended to.

The closed carriage, with fresh horses, was waiting. Lavina and the Earl hurriedly climbed aboard and they were on their way.

For the first part of the journey they each peered nervously out of a window, just in case the messenger returned to be sure his letter was delivered. But they saw nobody, and at last they began to relax.

"I can't believe that we're actually going to get away with this," the Earl murmured.

"We will if we keep our heads," Lavina told him. "And if the Marquis learns how to play his part properly."

"Why, whatever do you mean by that, my dear?"

"I'm talking about the way he refused to say goodbye to me. In fact, he put his hands behind him rather than touch me."

Her Father nodded and she continued,

"He spoke of behaving like a devoted fiancé – "

"Did he? I don't remember hearing him say that."

"It was while you were looking round the library. He said he would play his role with conviction – which, frankly, I doubt – and expected me to do the same."

"I suppose that's only reasonable. I'm afraid you will have to endure a certain amount of attention from him."

"Just as long as he doesn't try to kiss me," Lavina said, setting her chin stubbornly.

"I'm sure such an idea has never crossed his mind."

"Yes," she said crossly. "So am I. Did you see how he behaved when we left? It would be quite obvious, to anyone with any sense, that he was being forced into matrimony,

43

rather than begging me to honour him by becoming his wife."

The Earl sighed.

"I have to admit, my dear," he said, "that he does not play his part well. I'm not looking forward to this visit."

# CHAPTER FOUR

Their second arrival at Elswick Towers was as different from the first as anything could be. Clearly the Marquis had reflected that his earlier distant treatment of his 'fiancée' would not produce the desired effect, and had decided on a different approach.

He was there on the step to greet them, personally handing Lavina down from the carriage. Then, to her astonishment, he raised her hand to his lips, bending his head to kiss it with an air that would have looked like reverence to anyone who did not know the truth.

From behind him there came a great cheer from the assembled staff, lined up to greet the woman whom they supposed would be their new mistress.

"I didn't expect this – " she stammered.

"It is only proper that the future Marchioness of Elswick should receive suitable greetings from those over whom she will rule," he said smoothly.

"I – thank you." She tried to withdraw her hand, but he did not release it.

"You're supposed to look delighted by my attentions," he reminded her.

Lavina looked directly into his face, giving him the most dazzling smile at her command.

"My Lord," she breathed, "what joy it is to me to be

once again with you.   How my heart beats with happiness – "

"Be careful," he murmured, "don't overdo it."

"Can a woman overstate her pleasure at being in the presence of he who is to be her lord and master?"

Just for an instant the stone mask of his face seemed on the verge of cracking.   She almost thought a smile hovered on the edge of his lips.  But he mastered it.

"Your lord and master, indeed," he replied.   "I'm glad you understand that.  Now, my dearest love, let me introduce you to the staff that will be yours."

There were over a hundred of them, bowing or curtseying as she went along the line.

"I'm rather understaffed at the moment," the Marquis observed.   "As I said, this is a bachelor residence, and I do almost no entertaining.  Many of the people you see here work in the grounds or the stables.  Naturally, the presence of a Marchioness would make all the difference."

"Naturally," she murmured, feeling rather dazed.

"This is Perkins, the head butler, who runs this establishment."

Perkins, one of the few servants who had seen her earlier, bowed, concealing his bewilderment at this incredible development.

There were several under-butlers, then countless footmen, all powdered and wigged, each nodding his head to her.  There followed the under-footmen, and beyond them the chief cook, a magisterial French presence called Laurant, and two under-cooks.

There were, as the Marquis had said, several maids, smart in black dresses and gleaming white frilly aprons; also several scullery maids.  But there was no doubt that they were heavily outnumbered by the men.

"And now, allow me the pleasure of escorting you into

your new home," the Marquis said gallantly, taking her hand and leading her through the front door.

As soon as they were inside, Lavina said urgently.

"I must speak to you."

"Has something happened?"

"Yes, something terrible. The Queen has written to Papa."

"Saying what?"

"I don't know, I didn't allow him to open it."

"You didn't allow – ?"

"It would have been fatal," she said hurriedly, missing his implication. "Once he has read that letter he must obey the orders contained within it. As it is, he hasn't even received it."

"I thought you just said that he had."

"It arrived at the house, but we didn't."

He frowned.

"Didn't what?"

"Arrive at the house."

"Lady Lavina, you must forgive me for appearing dull-witted but I was under the impression that you had been home, and if you have not I'm at a loss to understand how you knew the letter was there."

"Of course we've been home."

The Marquis passed his hand over his eyes.

"Perhaps we began this conversation at the wrong point," he said faintly. "I have been used to starting at the beginning, but clearly you have devised another method."

Lavina stamped her foot.

"I wish you would stop talking nonsense. My meaning is perfectly clear."

"Not, unfortunately, to me. Did this letter arrive or did it not?"

47

"Yes, it arrived while we were here with you, and was waiting for us when we returned home. But Papa must not receive it, so I handed it back to the butler and we left at once.

"When the Queen's Messenger returns he will be informed that we never came back at all, and he must bring the letter on to deliver it here."

"Where he will find us all assembled to greet him," the Marquis said, his eye gleaming with appreciation. "Well done! Now that we have sorted out your somewhat tangled explanation, I am proud of you."

If he meant to placate Lavina by these words he was mistaken. Praise was pleasant, of course, but how dare he patronise her! Did he think she cared whether he was proud of her or not?

"Where are the maid and dresser you threatened me with?" the Marquis asked.

"They are following immediately. Since haste was important we left ahead of them."

"Then one of my maids shall show you to your room. You have the room always occupied by the mistress of the house."

Lavina soon discovered that what he called a 'room' was, in fact, a palatial apartment. Built on a corner, it had large windows on two sides, flooding it with light.

The furniture was all valuable, antique, but well kept. Dominating the room was a vast four poster bed, hung with honey coloured silk damask, and with a richly carved gold cornice.

Over the fireplace was a huge mirror set in a cream and gold frame that matched the bed. The ceiling too was a match. Everywhere Lavina looked she saw gold, from the chandelier to the chairs.

It was breathtaking. Evidently the Marchioness of

Elswick was expected to live in style.

The maid showed her around, pointing out the private bathroom, and the door that led to a dressing room.

One of the great windows looked out over the entrance, and to her relief Lavina saw the coach bringing her servants, followed by a fourgon piled with luggage.

"Thank goodness," she murmured.

She was more relieved than she could have said, for now she could employ her most formidable weapon in the strangest situation in which she had ever found herself. Her beauty, her glamour, her magnificence.

With these she could face the Marquis. And he would come off worse. She promised herself that.

*

Mrs Banty's entrance into her domain was made with almost as much ceremony as Lavina's. Dressed in black bombazine, her head adorned by a black straw bonnet, trimmed with black lace, she made a haughty progress up the grand staircase, and along the corridor to Her Ladyship's apartment.

Jill, Lavina's personal maid, crept along in the rear like a lady-in-waiting.

Behind them came troops of footmen bearing luggage, which they proceeded to set on the floor, until halted by a commanding voice.

"This will not do!"

"Banty dear, whatever is the matter?" Lavina asked.

"You cannot sleep here. It is disgraceful. I never heard of such a thing."

She looked sharply at the footmen, who were regarding her in amazement.

"What are you doing here? Take yourselves off, and somebody tell your master that I wish to see him without delay."

Their jaws dropped, and they looked at each other, wondering who was brave enough to inform the Marquis that a woman had sent for him as though he were an under-servant.

Luckily for everyone's peace of mind the Marquis himself put in an appearance at that moment. In seconds every footman in the place had vanished.

"I came to assure myself of your comfort," he said courteously to Lavina. "But I see your servants have arrived, and so all is well."

"All is certainly not well," Mrs Banty said, glaring at him. "I was never more shocked in my life."

Lavina held her breath, certain that this was disaster. The Marquis would never tolerate being spoken to in this manner, by a woman and a servant.

But instead of being offended he regarded Mrs Banty mildly.

"May I ask in what manner I have offended?" he asked.

"This apartment is totally inappropriate for Lady Lavina."

"It is the apartment of the mistress of the house. I meant to do her honour."

"But she is not yet the mistress of the house, and it is therefore scandalous for her to be in a bedroom that connects with your own."

"Indeed it does not," the Marquis said, astonished.

"It connects with this dressing room," Mrs Banty said, opening the door, and indicating another door on the far side of the dressing-room.

"Beyond that door lies Your Lordship's apartment," she said in a voice of thunder.

"Well yes," he agreed, "but you will observe that there are two beds in the dressing room, and I imagine that you will occupy one, and the maid will occupy the other.

"Were I to attempt to creep through this room with the intention of assaulting Lady Lavina's honour, I feel sure that you would prevent me. Besides, the door to my apartment is locked."

But Mrs Banty was made of stern stuff, and did not relent.

"I have no doubt that Your Lordship has a key."

"Which I shall be happy to give to you."

"How do I know that you don't have another key?"

"Very well," said the Marquis. "I will give you a pistol, and if you find me creeping through the dressing room you have my permission to shoot me."

Mrs Banty glared.

"Banty dear," begged Lavina, "please leave this. He's making fun of you."

"He *thinks* he is," Mrs Banty declared. "He thinks I wouldn't shoot him."

Incredibly, Lord Elswick's lips twitched.

"On the contrary," he said, "I feel fairly sure that you would. But if you would agree a compromise ma'am, suppose I send for the estate carpenter and instruct him to put some bolts on the door leading to my room. Once you have slid them home, Lady Lavina would be perfectly safe from my evil intentions."

Mrs Banty graciously signalled her assent to this negotiated settlement, and returned to her task, unpacking Lavina's wardrobe.

"My Lord, I apologise," Lavina said distractedly, anxious to protect her dresser from the Marquis' wrath, "Mrs Banty is very protective of me – "

"Do not," he said, his hand over his eyes, "even consider apologising for Mrs Banty. I would not have missed meeting her for the world."

"But the way she spoke to you – "

"Reminded me of my old governess. I was rather fond of her. Now I must hasten to give the order for those bolts. If she were to return and find the job not done, I would fear for my life."

"Ah, but you have not yet given her the pistol," Lavina reminded him, amused.

"I feel sure she has one of her own somewhere."

He hurried out, leaving Lavina looking after him, wondering at this man who kept revealing different sides of himself.

*

When the Earl collected his daughter to take her down to dinner his eyes popped with admiration.

"You look wonderful, my darling," he said.

"Doesn't she!" exclaimed Mrs Banty, who had every reason to be pleased with her work.

The gold of the room had inspired her to dress her darling in a dress of gold coloured satin, edged with a lavender ruche. Over this was a half skirt of lavender satin, and beneath the gold dress peeped a white silk petticoat with a white lace flounce.

At the back the dress fell away to a train, embroidered with sprays of purple and gold pansies. The bosom was cut low, not immodestly, but low enough to show the dainty diamond pendant. Lavender satin slippers and white gloves completed Lavina's appearance.

"My daughter is a credit to you, ma'am," said the Earl, who was always extremely polite to Mrs Banty, because he was afraid of her.

"Thank you, My Lord." The dresser accepted his tribute graciously, and melted away.

The Earl sighed with pleasure as he stood back to take another look at his daughter.

"There won't be a lady there to match you."

"There won't be any other ladies there at all, Papa," she said with a laugh.

"Oh but there will be. The Marquis has invited several other guests from the locality. There's the vicar, the mayor, and their wives, and I believe the rest are poor relations who live on the estate."

Lavina's mouth dropped open.

"I thought he never entertained like this."

"It seems he's made an exception."

"And bringing members of his family to meet me – "

"Well, he's doing it properly, which is very much to our purpose."

"Or his," Lavina thought. But she said nothing.

There was a knock on her door. Jill opened it, and admitted the Marquis.

He was splendidly dressed in black evening clothes, set off by a gleaming white embroidered shirt, at the top of which nestled a diamond pin.

Lavina had to tell herself not to stare. It crossed her mind that she had never seen a man look so handsome.

He inclined his head graciously in her direction.

"My compliments, ma'am," he said. "You are a bride of whom any man would be proud."

"I'm glad you feel that I'm a credit to you sir," Lavina replied with equal graciousness.

"There is only one thing needed to make your appearance perfect," he said. "Would you honour me by wearing these?"

Then she saw that he was carrying a large black box, which he opened, revealing the most astounding set of jewellery she had ever seen.

There was a necklace, a diadem, a bracelet, ear-rings, and two brooches, all in the most fabulous emeralds, set in gold.

"These are the Elswick emeralds," the Marquis explained. "Anyone seeing you wearing these will have to believe in the reality of the engagement."

He turned slightly to show the jewels to Mrs Banty.

"I should value your opinion ma'am," he said meekly.

"Very nice and suitable," she asserted.

"Which would you suggest for tonight?"

Mrs Banty considered.

"The necklace, the diadem and the ear-rings," she said.

"A bracelet?"

"That would be a little too much," she declared firmly.

"Then if you will be so good."

He stood back to allow Mrs Banty to do what was necessary.

When the jewellery was in place Lavina knew that she had never looked so magnificent. She looked, in fact, like a Marchioness.

"Some relatives of mine are here," the Marquis observed. "They will certainly recognise these jewels. If the Queen's messenger arrives I shall make sure that he too understands the implications, and – well, anyone else."

"Anyone else?" Lavina queried.

"I'm hoping that the local newspaper may send a representative. I told Hunsbury to drop a hint while he was there delivering the telegram, and he thinks it fell on fertile ground. If somebody tries to gatecrash, the doormen have been instructed to let them in."

There was no doubting it. Lavina had to admit that the Marquis was playing his part well.

Just before they departed the Earl murmured to his daughter,

"You two look very fine together, my dear."

And she murmured back,

"Papa, you have windmills in your head."

"Yes my dear, if you say so."

She went down to dinner on the Marquis' arm, to be introduced to the local dignitaries, and the relations. There were six of them, all elderly and thrilled be invited to Elswick Towers.

It was the Mayor's wife who told Lavina about Lord Elswick's kindness to them.

"They are really his pensioners, for he houses them and pays most of their bills," she confided. "Perhaps he did not tell you this, because he prefers people not to know of his kind actions."

"I'm beginning to understand that," Lavina murmured.

Of course she knew that his kindness had two edges. In return for his generosity he expected his relatives to be available when he needed them. But it was not lost on her that they all seemed genuinely fond of him, and spoke to him without fear.

One old lady in particular detained the Marquis with a long, detailed account of some domestic problem. He listened with every sign of interest, promised to send somebody to see to it and never once betrayed impatience.

Lavina grew even more curious about this man to whom she was officially betrothed.

At dinner she was seated beside him, and was made the recipient of many flattering attentions. Tomorrow morning, she guessed, the news would be spread far and wide, and all the time she and her Papa would be a little safer.

And yet, there was something very strange about it all.

The Earl was enjoying himself, having discovered two kindred spirits in the Mayor and his wife. They were both enthusiastic sailors, and as the Earl owned a yacht moored at Tilbury, and liked nothing better than to cruise in her, they were all soon deep in eager discussion.

"I've just had *The Mermaid* completely refitted," he said, "and, of course, redecorated."

"*The Mermaid*," sighed one of the lady relatives. "Such a lovely name!"

"We would normally have gone cruising in her this summer," the Earl explained, "but of course all plans are now in a state of abeyance."

"A cruise sounds an excellent idea," the Marquis said. "Perhaps we should think about it."

The talk drifted to other things. The vicar's wife wanted to know about the Queen. The Earl would have preferred not to discuss a subject that now filled him with dread, but he obliged with some innocent gossip about Her Majesty.

"Do you travel with her?" the Mayor asked.

"I have been to Osborne, on the Isle of Wight in attendance on Her Majesty," he replied. "But she travels very little, just Osborne, and Balmoral in Scotland."

"Scotland is such a beautiful place," sighed the vicar.

The Earl mentioned that he had a cousin who lived in Scotland, near Ballater, and for a while the talk was of the beauties of Scotland.

At last the Marquis rose to his feet.

But before he could speak the butler entered and murmured something in his ear. Lavina heard him say, "Send him in here."

When the butler had left, the Marquis addressed Lord Ringwood.

"The Queen's messenger has arrived for you."

The Earl blenched and seemed unable to speak.

Lavina, thinking quickly, said,

"I wonder what he can possibly want."

"I dare say you're used to being summoned to assist Her Majesty on important matters of state," said the vicar's wife breathlessly.

"Oh yes," said the Earl faintly.

"And it must be very urgent," pursued that lady, "to make him come here so late."

"Doubtless," the Earl managed to say.

"Perhaps it's a matter of national interest," she finished ecstatically.

This was so close to the truth that the Earl cast her a glance of horror, which made the vicar murmur in his wife's ear that this was really too worldly a discussion for such as themselves.

Both Lavina and her father recognised Sir Richard Peyton the man who entered the room. He was, as the Earl had called him, "a pale stick of a man", with no humour.

The Marquis received him graciously.

"You're just in time to join a toast to my bride," he said. "Lavina, my dear," he took her hand, raising her to her feet. "Was ever a man so fortunate?"

He handed Sir Richard a glass that a footman had filled.

"To Lady Lavina Ringwood, the future Marchioness of Elswick."

This put Peyton in an awkward position. He knew, as did everyone in the Queen's service, why Her Majesty required the presence of Lord Ringwood. He also knew that she was going to be, as he later put it to a crony, "ready to explode" when she heard of this engagement.

But he lacked the courage to refuse to drink the toast,

and he gulped down the champagne, praying that his royal mistress never found out, for she would certainly have his hide.

There were more toasts, speeches, and he was forced to delay his errand until everyone had left the table and repaired to the drawing room.

But then he was interrupted by the arrival of Mr. Ferris, a representative of the local newspaper, whom the Marquis cordially welcomed.

What was worse he spoke to Ferris for some minutes, and even introduced his bride, all of which made Sir Richard shiver as he thought of what would soon appear in the press.

Jack Ferris, who was the owner and editor of the local paper, could hardly believe his luck. To have gained admittance to Elswick Towers was more than he had hoped for, even after the strong hint he had been given earlier in the day.

Now the Marquis and Lady Lavina had greeted him affably.

"Come out into the garden," the Marquis invited him. "The fireworks are about to begin."

"Fireworks?" Lavina echoed.

"In your honour, my dear."

The French windows in the drawing room were thrown open and the company trooped out onto the broad terrace.

The Marquis took Lavina to stand in the centre of the broad stairs that led down to the lawns.

Darkness had fallen, and now the night sky was lit up by showers of glittering colour.

Most of the servants had come out into the garden to watch the firework display, and their "Oohs" and "Aaahs" blended in with the noises of the rockets.

Lavina stood at the top of the steps, her head raised to the sky, her attention absorbed in the gaudy beauty overhead.

She did not see that every eye was upon her. Nor did she see the Marquis turn his head and look at her for a long time.

As last she lowered her head and turned to look at him.

Then, to the cheers of the servants, and under the appalled eyes of Sir Richard and the fascinated eyes of Jack Ferris, the Marquis drew her close and laid his lips on hers.

It was the last thing she had expected from him, and she stood totally still with surprise.

It was not a fierce or passionate kiss. It was for the watching crowd, and it stayed well within the bounds of decorum. But the feel of his lips on hers was un-nerving.

His mouth was warm, firm, yet mobile, and it caressed hers gently. Lavina was intensely aware of the strength of his arms about her, and the feeling of his hard, wiry body against her.

"It would help if you looked a little enthusiastic," he murmured against her mouth.

"I – I can't – " she whispered, blushing.

"You are not playing your part, madam."

"I – very well."

Determinedly she put her arms about him, putting on a show of kissing him back. And then, somehow, she found that it was not a show, and she really was kissing him.

Shocked at herself, she drew back. Everyone around them was smiling, and she could see that he too was smiling. But it was a strange, uncertain smile, as though he were surprised at himself.

"Is that enthusiastic enough for you, sir," she asked demurely.

"It will do, for now."

They drew apart and, somehow, returned to normal. There were more toasts, champagne flowed.

Jack Ferris was still nearby, hastily scribbling. It was

clear that he had seen everything and would report everything, so Lavina supposed she should be very grateful to the Marquis.

But yet she wondered why a man should go to such lengths for something he had not wanted to do.

Emboldened, Jack Ferris approached her and said,

"Might I ask if the two of you have been acquainted for long?"

"For years," the Marquis said without hesitation. "In fact our first meeting was in London, at Lord Bracewell's house, is that not so, my love?"

"It was indeed," Lavina said promptly, "three years ago, although as I was not, strictly speaking, out at the time, perhaps it does not count as a proper meeting. But that was when we first set eyes on each other."

Ferris, overwhelmed with delight, scurried away to tell the world that Lord Elswick and his bride had long cherished a secret love.

Sir Richard regarded all this with a baleful eye, and wondered when he would be able to deliver his letter. At last he managed to approach the Earl, who had sufficiently recovered his nerve to smile and put the letter aside, saying,

"Have a drink, my dear fellow."

"Lord Ringwood, it is of the highest importance that you read this now. Her Majesty urgently requires your presence tomorrow at Windsor Castle."

Reluctantly the Earl opened and read the letter, which did, indeed, summon him in imperious tones, 'to discuss a matter of national importance'.

But then the Marquis looked over his shoulder, saying,

"You can't do that, old fellow. We'll have started on our cruise by then."

To Sir Richard he explained,

"Lord Ringwood and Lady Lavina have invited me for a trip on their yacht, and we leave immediately. So he will be unable to accept the Queen's kind invitation."

"It is not an invitation," said the startled Sir Richard. "It is a summons."

"Whatever it is, Lord Ringwood cannot attend, as we are headed for the sea tomorrow morning."

The Marquis slapped Sir Richard on the back and spoke with terrifying geniality.

"Her Majesty will have to wait until he gets back. It can't be that important."

Sir Richard was beyond speech. His eyes seemed to pop out of his head.

"Have another drink," the Marquis told him. "I've had a room prepared for you."

Sir Richard began to protest that he must return to Windsor Castle, but he reflected that an overnight stay would give him a chance to talk Lord Ringwood into doing his duty, and yielded.

Soon after that the party ended. A stream of carriages pulled away from the front door, and Sir Richard went unhappily to bed.

"Let us go into the library," the Marquis said to the other two.

With the doors safely closed behind them, he said,

"We have to decide on a plan of action."

"It's useless," the Earl moaned. "What can we do? Tomorrow he will refuse to leave without me."

"He can't do so if you've already left," the Marquis pointed out. "We told him that we were going to join your ship, and that's what we must do."

"But where will we sail?" Lavina asked.

"Where do you normally go?"

"The Mediterranean."

"But I don't think we should go there," the Earl said anxiously. "Too close to the Balkans."

"I agree," the Marquis said. "So perhaps we should head for Scotland? I believe I heard you mention that you have family there, near Ballater. It's a logical destination."

"But isn't Ballater near Balmoral?" Lavina reminded them. "And the Queen goes there in summer."

"But not for another month," the Earl said. "We can have left Scotland by then. It's the perfect solution, except – oh dear. My Captain will not be expecting us."

"Leave that to me," said the Marquis. "Then it's settled that we leave tomorrow, as early as possible."

# CHAPTER FIVE

Whatever the Marquis planned he carried out efficiently, or at least got Hunsbury to carry out for him.

The Earl found himself awakened at an early hour by Hunsbury wanting his "instructions for the telegram."

The Earl, who had not known that he was going to send a telegram, stared.

"The local Post Office will telegraph the Tilbury Post Office, who will take it to your Captain, so that he will know you are arriving."

"Oh my goodness!" the Earl exclaimed. "The wonders of modern science. Whatever will they think of next."

He and Lavina joined the Earl for a very early breakfast. Through the window they could see the trunks being loaded and the carriage brought round.

"I think we might depart now," said the Marquis, finishing his coffee.

"But what about Sir Richard," the Earl asked. "Surely I must speak to him before I leave?"

"Do you know, I think it might be better if you did not," the Marquis murmured. "I have left a letter to be delivered to him when he wakes, offering my apologies for whisking you away."

"In that case," the Earl said decidedly, "let us be gone immediately."

The carriage took them as far as the railway station where they boarded the train that would take them to Tilbury.

"I cannot believe that this is happening," said Lavina when the train was moving.

The Marquis had gone out into the corridor, leaving them alone to talk.

"It does seem incredible," the Earl agreed. "Two days ago we had no idea that any of this was possible. And now, here we are, headed for the coast. I do hope we have a calm sea for our voyage."

"I hope so, too. Although, on the whole, I think I'm a good sailor."

"You have been one ever since you were three years old, when I took you on the yacht, and you ran from cabin to cabin. Of course you were terribly spoilt by the crew, who thought you adorable."

"Which I was," Lavina answered with a smile.

"You certainly were, and you have been even more adorable ever since. I cannot think what I would do without you."

Lavina knew what was in his mind, by a sudden sadness in his voice.

"You are thinking of Mama," she said gently, "and how wretched you were when she died."

He nodded.

"I loved your mother from the first time I saw her, and she gradually fell in love with me. It took a little time and a little ingenuity to make her love me, but when she did so, it was with her whole heart and soul. We were very happy. Do you remember that?"

"Of course. That's why, when I was young, I was happy, too. The house never seemed quite the same after Mama died, and I still miss her very much, even though it is four years since she left us."

"I miss her too," the Earl said. "I will miss her even more when you leave me. How dark and lonely the house will be without you."

"But Papa, what are you saying? I'm not really getting married. Eventually this 'engagement' will end, and we will go on as before."

"I wonder if it will be so easy. Suppose the Queen cannot find another bride to take your place?"

"I hope she doesn't. Why should I wish on another woman the fate I don't want for myself? She will have to find some other way, that doesn't involve marrying some poor creature off like selling a head of cattle."

"You're right of course. I only mean that she may continue to apply pressure for some time, and that would make it hard for you to break the engagement. You might even have to go through with the marriage."

Lavina laughed.

"Have no fear, Papa. Lord Elswick would find that idea as horrifying as I should myself."

The train had slowed now so that there was much less noise and Lavina's voice carried clearly.

It carried to Lord Elswick standing outside in the corridor, and, since there was nobody to see him, he allowed himself a private smile.

*

Nothing surprised Lord Ringwood more than arriving at Tilbury to discover that the Captain of his vessel was ready for him, having received the telegram.

The boat, which despite being called a yacht was actually powered by steam engines, was looking exceedingly smart.

Lavina was delighted to see her father had had the inside decorated in a pale blue.

The Captain greeted them heartily, and told the Earl that he would be pleased with the crew, and with the refitted engines.

As guest of honour, the Marquis was given the Master Cabin. As soon as he was settled in and all the baggage was aboard the Captain gave the order to cast off.

As they moved slowly out of port, Lavina watched the shore recede. After a moment the Marquis came to stand beside her.

"Are you easier in your mind now?" he asked.

"Oh yes. They cannot catch us. How will they know where to look? Your butler will not tell anyone."

"I instructed him to say that we were going to the Mediterranean. On the other hand – "

He looked into the distance.

"Is that not a naval gunship I see pursuing us?"

"*What?*" she cried. "Oh no, please no – where?"

"Nowhere, you goose. I was joking."

Her hands flew to her mouth and she choked back a sob.

"That was unkind," she said. "You don't know how I dread – "

"Then forgive me. I did not mean to distress you. But aren't you forgetting that I have promised to protect you at all costs?"

"Yes, and I am sure you mean it, but – "

"But you still fear the Queen? Do not. You can back me to defeat her any day."

Then, as though seeming to feel that he had been kindly for long enough, he resumed his brusque manner and announced that he intended to join her father and the Captain on the bridge, and he would see her at dinner.

It was already late in the day so dinner would be the only meal before it was time to retire.

Over dinner the Marquis produced a surprise.

"*The Times!*" Lavina exclaimed. "However did you come by it, for I know we left too early to receive it at your home."

"I sent my valet out hunting for it as soon as we reached Tilbury," Lord Elswick said. "The announcement is in there, together with a short piece by Mr. Ferris. The telegraph wires must have been humming last night."

Lavina looked and saw, in bold type. *The engagement is announced –*

"By now I dare say the Queen will have seen it," the Marquis observed. "I cannot help feeling that we were wise to flee."

"By the time I have to see her again, she will be used to the idea," the Earl said, feeling brave now that he was at sea.

For the rest of dinner Lavina took very little part in the conversation, and was content to have it so. It pleased her to see that her father and the Marquis were talking pleasantly together.

By the time the meal was finished he was looking almost like an agreeable man.

He was also, she thought, much more handsome than when he was scowling and being aloof.

She bade the men goodnight, meaning to go to bed early. She knew her father would come to her cabin to kiss her goodnight.

He was, in fact, later than she expected. When he did come she said,

"Oh, Papa, I thought perhaps you had forgotten me."

"I was talking to our guest," her father replied. "You'll be surprised to learn that he is an expert on foreign countries. He was telling me of the strange places he has visited in the East."

"Yes, I am surprised at that."

"I think his mind is more wide-ranging than we gave him credit for. I certainly think he has wasted his life buttoned up in his castle, and treating women as if they were poison."

Lavina laughed.

"I only hope he does not push me overboard when I am least expecting it," she said.

"For shame to speak of him like that, when you owe him so much!" her father said with a smile. "Perhaps he'll become more human and enjoy life, as he should do, by the time this trip is over."

"I think, Papa, anyone who is with you, would be enjoying what they were doing. You have to admit that the yacht had never looked or moved so well as it is doing at the moment."

Her father smiled.

"You are right," he agreed, "and he admires *The Mermaid* very much."

"No wonder you suddenly find him more agreeable," Lavina laughed.

"Well, if his mood softens he may take a brighter view of life in general. Perhaps he'll find Scottish women attractive."

Lavina laughed.

"It's no use being optimistic, although, of course, I've always been told that the girls in the highlands are very attractive."

"No one is more attractive than you, my darling. If the Marquis is too stupid to realise that, we can only hope that he enjoys haggis instead.

"Mind you," he added, "I think he *does* realise it – "

"You are mistaken, Papa. That kiss was for show."

The Earl sighed.

"I only wanted to say how much I admired your endurance, my dear. And how much I pitied you."

"Pitied me, Papa?" Lavina was startled.

"You told me on the way here how averse you were to the idea that he might kiss you."

"Oh – oh yes, I did say that, didn't I?" she said, trying to remember it, and wondering what she had been thinking of.

"And when he did so, I thought your fortitude was much to be commended."

Lavina pulled herself together.

"We all have to make sacrifices, Papa."

"And you made yours nobly." He patted her hand. "But would you like me to have a quiet word with him, to make sure that he doesn't do such a thing again?"

"I don't think so, Papa dear," she said quickly. "It wouldn't be very polite, would it, when he is doing so much for us?"

"You're quite right," the Earl agreed solemnly. "And if it should happen again – well, you will just have to be brave about it."

"Whatever you say, Papa."

"Goodnight, my dear."

The Earl kissed her goodnight before leaving the cabin, closing the door quietly behind him.

Lavina cuddled down under the sheets, with a blissful feeling that the boat carrying her across the water was leaving all her problems behind.

She fell asleep with a smile on her lips.

*

Next day she spent much of her time looking over the ship's rail, knowing that they were moving ever closer to Aberdeen, the nearest port to Ballater, where her unknown Scottish relatives lived.

The Earl had shown Lavina the letter from his cousin, inviting them to arrive at any time. Even so, she wondered how they would feel at a visit with no warning.

That evening, as soon as dinner was over, she once more left her father and the Marquis to get to know each other, which they seemed to be doing really well.

But instead of going to her cabin she stood watching the distance lights from the shore, for now they were travelling close enough to the shore to see it most of the time.

Just a few yards away from this part of the boat was the Music Room. It was Lavina's mother who had insisted on putting a small piano in the saloon, for Lavina's sake.

The little girl had always loved the music her mother played for her. Her father used to hold her hands and make her dance to the tunes.

She smiled now thinking of those happy memories that would stay with her always.

Closing her eyes, she conjured up the sound of a piano in her mind, seeing her mother sitting there, dreamily playing a dance tune. It was called 'The Summer Waltz', and the child had loved it.

"Again, Mama, again!" she had cried, clapping her hands in glee.

And Mama had played it for her as often as she wanted.

As she grew older Lavina had learned to play the violin, and an instrument was kept on board for her. There had been such joy in playing with dear Mama. And then Mama had died, and the joy had died with her.

Suddenly Lavina opened her eyes. She was not dreaming. Somebody really was playing 'The Summer Waltz' on the piano, just as her mother had once done.

She crept along the corridor and quietly opened the door of the music room, wondering who could play so well.

And there, to her astonishment, she saw the Marquis sitting at the piano.

His back was to the door, so that he had no idea that anyone was listening to him.

It had never, for one moment, occurred to her that this harsh man might be musical. But perhaps, she thought, the solitary life he had chosen had made him turn to music as a way of assuaging his loneliness.

For a moment she stood in the doorway hesitating.

Then she slipped across the carpet without making a sound and sat down in one of the chairs. For an hour she sat very still and silent, listening to him with deep pleasure as he played a large spectrum of pieces, sad, joyful, sweet and melancholy.

It seemed to Lavina that his soul was in every note. In this way he could communicate, but apparently in no other way, and she began to feel sad for him.

Then she realised that he had started to play 'The Summer Waltz' again. Moving as though she could not prevent herself, she reached into the low cupboard where her violin was kept, and quietly drew it out.

Very slowly and very softly she began to play, joining in with the Marquis. There was the briefest possible hesitation in his playing, but then he continued, without looking round. She wondered if he guessed who had joined him.

When the music came to an end she waited for him to turn and speak to her. But he remained still, and now it occurred to her that he might be angry at her intrusion.

Perhaps he thought that if he ignored her, she might go away.

Then, just as she was deciding that this might be the best thing to do, the Marquis turned round and looked at her with an expression in his eyes that she had never seen from him before.

"So it's you," he said in a quiet, almost wondering voice. "I couldn't imagine who it was whose musicianship seemed so much a part of my own. I did not know that you could play the violin."

Lavina laughed.

"And I had no idea that you could play the piano," she replied.

"I have played since I was very young," the Marquis told her. "Now I live alone, I find there is no company so consoling as the piano."

"I feel the same about the violin," she said. "I can also play the piano."

"You can?" he exclaimed. "From what your father has told me about you I thought of you as being an outdoor girl, liking only riding horses."

"I do enjoy those things," Lavina told him, "but I find that music is almost as thrilling and exciting as jumping a high fence."

The Marquis looked at her with new interest.

"What a fascinating comparison. But then, you're a very unusual young woman, in every way. If you were not, I suppose we wouldn't be here, on this boat together. I've thought of you as many things, but never before as musical."

"Nor I, you," she said. "But now I know why you don't feel lonely when you are at the castle."

Even as she spoke she realised she had said the wrong thing. Immediately the Marquis turned and started to play another popular tune, a very fast one, this time. It was almost, Lavina thought, like someone dancing wildly and madly to prevent him or herself thinking of what they had lost or what was impossible to possess.

Just for a moment she hesitated.

Then, as she knew the tune, she began to play it with him, matching him speed for speed, and knowing that she was playing extremely well. He gave her a quick glance and upped the tempo. She managed to stay with him, and they rattled away together until the tune came to a triumphant finish.

As the last notes died away he looked at her, his eyes alight with satisfaction.

"That might have come from the Albert Hall," he said. "Perhaps one day, if we were to lose all we possess we might get ourselves hired there."

Lavina laughed.

"Thank you for the compliment."

"You deserve it. You play extremely well and I can only think you were taught by a very experienced musician."

"Actually, it was my mother who wanted me to play, to please my father," Lavina told him. "I have loved music ever since I heard the first note when I was in the cradle."

He was silent for a moment, before nodding in agreement.

"Music makes me forget all grief and woe," he said. "When I play I pass into another world, one that has never been spoilt."

For a moment Lavina could not think of an answer.

After a pause she said:

"Play me one of your favourite songs and I will see if I know it well enough to join in with you."

The Marquis turned towards the piano and began to play a gentle, yearning piece of music that, for all its slow tempo, was very difficult. For a few ecstatic minutes they played as one.

When the last note had died away he rose from the piano and looked at her, as though something about her puzzled him.

"I didn't think it possible that I would find someone

with whom I am so much in harmony, whose music seemed to come from the same well-spring as my own."

Lavina was silent for a moment, thinking the answer to this was very obvious. He had spent too much time alone, seldom visiting other houses, and not knowing of the music that was made in them.

Suddenly he seemed to become aware of how he was talking to her. She could almost see him withdraw back into himself. He turned towards the door, saying abruptly,

"Goodnight, I hope you sleep well."

Before she could answer, he had shut the door behind him.

Lavina was left alone. She was aware that the yacht had also come to a standstill, presumably in some quiet bay where it would rest until tomorrow morning.

"Goodnight," she said to an empty room.

Then as there was only the sound of the waves lapping against the sides, she walked quietly, without seeing anyone, or being seen, towards her own cabin.

Jill was waiting for her. She helped her off with her lovely clothes and into her elegant silk nightdress, then began to brush her long dark hair.

"Did you have an enjoyable evening, Your Ladyship?" she asked.

"Yes thank you, Jill. It was certainly a very – a very unexpected evening."

Before Jill could ask what she meant by that Lavina said hurriedly, "You can go to bed now. I'll manage the rest for myself."

She sat alone, slowly drawing the brush down her hair, thinking what a strange discovery she had made that night.

"If anyone had told me he was like this, I would not have believed them," she said to herself.

"I thought he was just rude and brusque, but there is another side to him, a side that I can reach, and which seems to be reaching out to me."

She got into bed and lay gazing into the darkness, listening to the soft murmuring of the sea. Then she fell asleep, only to dream, as she had dreamed before, that the music was whispering in her heart, and as her mother always said, in her soul.

*

The next day they docked in Aberdeen. From there they went to the railway station and began the train journey to Ballater.

Remote as the location was, it was well supplied with railways on account of its nearness to Balmoral, the Scottish country estate that Queen Victoria and Prince Albert had acquired twenty years before.

During the Prince's lifetime they had spent a part of each summer there. After his death Victoria had continued the visits alone.

At Ballater Station they piled into carriages to head for the McEwuan estate. Lavina was thrilled to see how beautiful the Scottish countryside was.

The green of the grass, the touches of heather were something new and thrilling.

She felt she was entering a new world which, thankfully, was not as frightening nor as difficult as the world in the south had become.

"What is the house like?" the Marquis asked.

"It's called McEwuan Castle," the Earl replied, "and it is somewhat like a castle, but not as grand as the Towers."

"That's a relief," the Marquis said at once. "I still lose my way in that huge place. I hope your cousin has a cool head, or he will be overwhelmed at our descending on him without warning."

"But we do have an invitation from him to drop in at any time," the Earl pointed out. "I received it only three days ago."

"But Papa," Lavina laughed, "when people say that, they never mean it literally."

"Then he shouldn't have said it," the Earl replied. "We are visiting them as an act of courtesy, to mark your betrothal."

"Then they are to believe that we are really engaged?" the Marquis asked.

"Would that not be best?" the Earl asked.

"Certainly. The fewer people who know the truth the better."

At last McEwuan Castle came into view. It was not a great castle, but it had towers and turrets, and presented a very romantic appearance.

"There is my cousin!" the Earl exclaimed suddenly.

A large, well-built man came out of the front door and stood regarding them as they approached. His face wore a big grin, and he waved to them, not seeming in the least put out by their sudden appearance.

"Ian!" the Earl called out.

Sir Ian McEwuan hurried forward so that he reached the carriage as it stopped. Without waiting for the coachman he pulled open the door, grabbed his cousin by the hand and almost yanked him out to a crushing embrace.

"So you decided to accept my invitation, after all! This is wonderful! *Come on out everybody! They're here after all this time!*"

The last words were directed inside the house, and at once a young man came running out. He was very good-looking and seemed only a little older than Lavina.

"This is my son, Andrew," Sir Ian said. "Now, Andrew, here is your Cousin Edward, whom you haven't met since you were very young, and your Cousin Lavina whom you've never met at all."

By this time the coachman had handed Lavina down, and the Marquis had followed. Now he was standing watching the commotion with an expression of faint amusement.

The young man held out his hand.

"Cousin Edward, Cousin Lavina, it's wonderful to meet you at last."

Then the Earl suddenly remembered they had a guest with them and said,

"I want you to meet our guest, the Marquis of Elswick, who has come with us to Scotland. He wants to see if it is as wonderful as we have told him."

This remark was very well received. The McEwuans ushered them joyfully through the front door into the castle.

"Welcome! Welcome!" Sir Ian said to them all. "I've been hoping for years that you would come and visit me. Now, almost as if you had dropped down from heaven, you have arrived."

"We are very pleased to be here," the Earl replied. "As we left England unexpectedly we didn't have the time to warn you of our arrival."

"We need no warning," Sir Ian said. "This is Scotland. The door is always open to friends and family."

Sir Ian took them up the stairs to what Lavina thought must be the drawing-room where their hostess was waiting to receive them.

She was a handsome woman in her early fifties, with red hair and a smiling face.

"This is a great surprise," she said to the Earl, "but a delightful one. I'm having rooms prepared for you at once, and in the mean time, let us have sherry."

Looking around, Lavina realised that the inside of the

house was charming, and far more comfortable and pretty than she had expected. She had thought that because it was in the far north, that the house would be somewhat chilly and austere.

Instead she found everywhere comfortably furnished with pictures which she was sure were very valuable. There were curtains and carpets which would have been acceptable in any drawing-room in Mayfair.

"I do hope that you'll stay long enough for our friends to meet you," Lady McEwuan said.

"We want to see as much of Scotland as we can," Lavina said.

"But we have another reason for coming," the Earl added. "And that is, to announce the engagement of Lord Elswick to my daughter."

Everyone expressed their delight. There were toasts and more toasts. The Marquis stood beside Lavina, receiving congratulations with an air of ease, but she wondered how this felt to him.

Even after last night, when they had played music together and she had felt a sweet communication between them, she had no insight into his mind.

He had withdrawn into himself again. Although his manner this morning was coolly friendly, the wonderful moment might never have been.

Yet now he played his part to perfection, apparently the devoted fiancé. But when she looked into his eyes, she saw nothing there.

# CHAPTER SIX

Dressing for dinner that evening, Lavina took great care about her appearance. She wanted to make an excellent impression on her new relatives.

It was only when she went downstairs that she discovered that there were other guests for dinner, who had been out fishing that day.

"Cousin Lavina," said Andrew, "let me introduce my friend, Sir James McVein, whose estate runs next to this one."

Sir James was six feet tall and had been, she learnt later, in the army until he came into his father's title. He had then retired to look after his very large estate.

She found herself sitting next to him at dinner, and realised that he was definitely one of the best looking young men she had ever seen. Also one of the most amusing.

He kept her laughing by telling her the things which had happened in the north since he had served in the army and the difficulties he had encountered since he became a land owner.

"My father was Scottish and my mother was English," he told Lavina. "So when I have a problem to solve I ask myself which will be the most sensible or the most valuable."

Lavina laughed.

"One always gets back to money in the south," she

replied. "I am sure people in the north are the same, although I expect you to be more patriotic."

"I think we are patriotic," the Scotsman agreed. "At the same time we try to be sensible and not in any way so easily aroused to anger as our ancestors were."

Lavina laughed again.

"As far as I remember, the history of Scotland is full of battles and I have always felt I should be careful in case I insulted anyone, and suffered in consequence."

Sir James smiled.

"I think you are quite safe," he said. "I assure you the Scots love beauty, whether it is a flower or a woman. You will find yourself admired wherever you go."

Lavina blushed.

"Thank you," she said. "Now I will not be so frightened of saying or doing the wrong thing."

"Then Scotland welcomes you with open arms," he replied. "I will give a party immediately in your honour at my own house."

"I shall be delighted to accept," she said. "And so, of course, will my fiancé."

"Your fiancé?" he asked in dismay.

Then she realised that he had not been there for the announcement of her engagement.

"Tell me it isn't true," he said. "This is an imaginary fiancé."

"No, he's sitting over there, next to Lady McEwuan, Lord Elswick."

There was silence. Then the young man said,

"That makes me more sad than I can say."

As he spoke Lavina looked up into his eyes. She felt for a moment as if they held her captive.

Then she blushed and turned away, feeling that something strange and unusual had happened.

In the following days the whole neighbourhood opened its arms to them. There were dinners, lunches, dances. Something happened every night.

Sir James invited them to his estate, so that he could show them his horses which, everyone agreed, were the best for miles around.

The Marquis seemed to think so too, for he studied the horses with admiration, and spent a long time discussing them with Sir James. Nobody noticed that now and then the Marquis regarded him with cool hostility that sat oddly with his friendly words.

Lavina, glancing across at them from a few yards away, saw only that the Marquis seemed at ease, and was reassured.

When she was alone with her father she could not help saying to him,

"You know, Papa, I think this visit to Scotland is doing us all a great deal of good, but most especially the Marquis. He is becoming almost human."

Her father laughed.

"What do you mean by that?" he asked.

"You know exactly what I mean," Lavina replied. "He was laughing and talking about the horses and going from one to another. He found them as marvellous as we did and I thought he was becoming almost human."

"He was certainly very amusing at dinner last night after the ladies had left the room," the Earl said. "He told us stories which I had never heard before and some of the jokes, while not for female ears, were extremely witty and amusing."

Lavina stared.

"Lord Elswick knows jokes that are unfit for females?" she echoed. "I don't believe you, Papa."

"My dear, every gentleman knows jokes that are unfit for females," her father declared firmly.

"Good heavens! You too?"

"I do after listening to Elswick last night," he said mischievously.

Sir James produced a dainty, spirited little mare for Lavina to ride, and accompanied her on a short trip around his grounds.

"We'll go for a longer ride together tomorrow," he said. "At least, I hope you'll want to."

"But are you not going fishing tomorrow?" Lavina asked. "I'm sure that Papa and Lord Elswick – "

"They're going fishing," Sir James answered. "But I'm not."

The expression in his eyes made Lavina look away because she was blushing.

"I – I don't think I can," she said, wishing she were free to flirt with this handsome young man.

"You could if you really wanted to," he said. "Surely your 'lord and master' would not object to an innocent ride?"

"My lord and master?" she echoed in astonishment. "Whoever do you mean?"

"You told me that you were betrothed to Lord Elswick."

"Which makes him my fiancé, not my lord and master."

"Isn't it the same thing?"

"Certainly not!" she said indignantly.

"But does he see it that way? To my eyes he looks like a tyrannical kind of man."

"I do not permit him to order me around," Lavina said loftily.

"Then you'll come riding with me tomorrow?"

"Yes, I will."

Impulsively he seized her hand and kissed it.

Despite her confident words Lavina was a little unsure exactly how Lord Elswick would react. So that evening, just before everyone went up to bed, she wished him a good day's fishing, and informed him that she would be riding with Sir James McVein.

"I hope you enjoy the day, ma'am."

"You do not object?"

"Why should I? You will of course be properly accompanied by a groom – "

"Well, I – "

"In fact, I'll mention it to Sir Ian immediately." He gave her a smile. "Just in case you should happen to forget."

He went off immediately to speak to Sir Ian, and returned with the news that two of the McEwuan daughters would also be accompanying them.

Then he told her that he hoped she would sleep well, and went up stairs, leaving her fuming.

The following day she and Sir James set out on horseback, accompanied by Isabel and Geraldine McEwuan, and a groom. At the end of an extremely dull day she returned home, in a mood to quarrel.

She was unable to quarrel with the Marquis, however, as he was not there. The gentlemen arrived home while she was dressing for dinner.

As always the table was enlarged by several neighbours, one of whom, Eglantine McCaddy, was the local beauty, also known for her singing.

At dinner she had the honour of being seated next to the Marquis, who paid her a great deal of flattering attention, seemingly entranced by her charms.

For the life of her, Lavina could not see what he found to admire. To her the 'beauty' seemed overblown and vulgar, her attractions obvious, her laughter too noisy.

And this was the man who loathed and abominated women, bowing down before this coarse temptress, while his fiancée looked on!

Her singing was no better. Her voice was loud, which was about the best that could be said for it. Why the Marquis had to insist on accompanying her was beyond Lavina.

Somehow it was this that upset her most. His piano playing had been a secret between them, hinting at a greater closeness, possible in the future. By revealing it to the world he had mysteriously devalued it, and that hurt her more than she wanted to admit.

When the performance was over there was loud applause, which the two performers received with a theatrical simulation of modesty that made Lavina want to throw something at one – or both – of them.

As the party repaired for the night the Marquis drew Lavina aside for a private word. There was a glint in his eyes that might have been amusement, or perhaps something more disturbing.

"Are you angry with me?" he asked.

"I have every reason to be – carrying on like that in front of everyone."

"At least I didn't kiss her hand, or try to slip away for a private tryst, as you attempted."

"We were going riding," she snapped.

"To be sure you were! Did you enjoy it?"

She glowered at him.

"What do you see in him, Lavina?"

"He is charming company," she said stiffly.

"And I'm not. I'm a curmudgeon with rough manners. But it was to me that you turned for help, because the very qualities that make me a disaster in society make me strong enough to help you.

"You cannot have it both ways. If you are falling in love with that man then say so. I'll withdraw my suit and leave you to him."

"Oh no, you mustn't – "

"But I will if you give me cause. Think about it. Perhaps an engagement to him would serve your purpose just as well."

"I do not wish to be engaged to him," she said with soft vehemence.

"Just to flirt with him? I see. Let me warn you against that. I will not be made a fool of. *Do you understand me?*"

"Yes."

"Good. In that case I will bid you goodnight."

He walked ahead without a backward look, leaving her to run to her room, throw herself on the bed and thump the pillow.

\*

Despite this, life moved on fairly contentedly for another week. Lavina was entranced by the beauties of Scotland, and when she rode it was mostly at Lord Elswick's side. When not annoyed he was good company.

She was almost allowing herself to relax and push her fears aside, when, one morning, Lady McEwuan came rushing into the drawing room, full of excitement.

"There's a carriage coming up the drive, and it has the royal crest on the panels."

Lavina's blood ran cold, and her frantic eyes sought her father's.

He rose to his feet, pale but determined. The family would have followed him, but Sir Ian said firmly,

"It will be confidential business from Her Majesty. We will not intrude."

Holding each other's hand for comfort, the Earl and

Lavina went out into the hall to greet whoever should appear. The front door was pulled open.

"Papa," Lavina said in horror, "Look who it is!"

The man who appeared was Sir Richard Peyton, the same man that they had deluded and left behind at The Towers. Lavina and father exchanged alarmed glances, wondering what he could be doing here.

Sir Richard approached them, his face rigid, paused and gave a small, curt nod.

"What are you doing this far north, Peyton?" the Earl asked with an attempt at geniality.

"I am with Her Majesty at Balmoral," the man replied stiffly.

"Balmoral?" The Earl exclaimed. "It's too early in the year for that. The Queen never comes north until next month."

"Her Majesty has decided to make an exception this year," Sir Richard declared. "She has a special guest who particularly wished to see the glories of Scotland."

Lavina felt as though the world had stood still. There was a strange ringing in her ears, and suddenly she was full of dread.

"What – special guest?" Lord Ringwood asked in a hollow voice.

Sir Richard drew himself up until he was practically standing to attention. In a loud voice he announced,

"Her Majesty has been pleased to invite Lord Ringwood, and his daughter, Lady Lavina Ringwood, to a reception tomorrow evening, at which they will have the honour of meeting Prince Stanislaus of Kadradtz."

A ghastly silence greeted this pronouncement. Sir Richard then handed over the invitation card.

"But – er – " the Earl stammered, "Is there not another invitation, for Lord Elswick?"

"Her Majesty is unaware of Lord Elswick's presence in the neighbourhood, and has therefore not been able to include him on the list."

"But now that she is aware – "

A shout of laughter interrupted him. Everyone turned to look at the Marquis strolling into the hall, his face alight with hilarity.

"It's no use, Ringwood," he said. "Wild horses wouldn't persuade the Queen to acknowledge my presence if it meant inviting me to a reception to which, in any case, I do not wish to attend."

At the sight of the Marquis Sir Richard drew himself up.

"My Lord, I consider you treated me most shabbily at our last meeting."

"No choice. Anyway, you seem to have got your own back. I wonder how the Queen knew where we were?"

Sir Richard glared at him.

"You told her, of course, and how did you know where we were?" the Marquis mused.

"Your butler was as misleading as you instructed him to be," Sir Richard said stiffly.

"But you managed to bribe some of the others, I suppose. I dare say there was one listening at the library key-hole the night before. Well, I hope Her Majesty rewards you for it, but I doubt it. She doesn't like sneaks any more than I do, even though she isn't above using their services. You can leave now."

"I have to take back an answer."

"The answer will be delivered without help from you. Take yourself off."

Catching the Marquis' baleful eye Sir Richard scuttled away into his carriage.

"I can't go to this reception without you," Lavina said

urgently. "You know what the Queen is doing, don't you?"

"Certainly I do, and there is no fear of your going without me. You may safely leave this in my hands."

"At least tell me what you mean to do."

"There is not the slightest necessity for you to know," he informed her with a touch of loftiness. "When I tell you that I shall take care of the problem, you may be assured that all is well."

Lavina's eyes kindled.

"You're very high-handed, sir."

"Indeed I am. You have always known as much."

"I only meant – "

"I know very well what you meant. You knew what I was like when we began this venture. It's too late to complain now. Ringwood, it is my intention to call upon Her Majesty. I suggest that you come with me."

Lord Ringwood paled.

"But the Queen is not expecting us," he protested.

"Her Majesty is well known for appreciating informality when at Balmoral," the Marquis replied smoothly. "She will be overjoyed at a visit from her neighbours."

Lord Ringwood only wished he could be as certain, but the Marquis was in a determined mood.

"At least tell me what you intend to say to her," Lavina insisted.

The Marquis regarded her with a touch of humour.

"I think I had better not tell you," he said. "You might explode with rage."

He walked away without a backward glance, leaving Lavina glaring after him.

Half an hour later the carriage departed for Balmoral, bearing the Earl and the Marquis, both superbly dressed as befitted men who were about to enter the royal presence.

It would be hours before they could return, and the thought of twiddling her thumbs was intolerable. Lavina rushed upstairs to put on her riding habit, took a horse from the stables and went for a long ride.

When she returned there was still no sign of them, so she began pacing up and down, grinding her nails into her palms. She was a prey to the most violent agitation, but whether it sprang from fear for her father, for herself, or from annoyance at Lord Elswick, she could not quite decide.

If only they would hurry up and come home!

At last she saw the carriage appear in the distance, heading for home. She controlled her impatience until both men were walking into the house.

"All is well, my dear," the Earl said, embracing her. "Lord Elswick will be coming to Balmoral with us tomorrow night."

"But do not tell your daughter how I arranged it," the Marquis murmured, "until I am safely out of throwing distance."

Lavina took her father's arm and marched him into the garden.

"Papa, what has he done?"

"Oh my dear, if only you could have seen him! He was magnificent, the way he stood up to the Queen. He insisted on the Chamberlain announcing us, and when we walked in he greeted her, and said he knew that she would wish to congratulate him on his betrothal to you."

"The Queen was very taken aback, but she recovered and actually declared that there was no betrothal, as you were a member of the royal family, and could not marry without her consent."

"*Papa!*"

"You will never believe what he replied."

"I'd believe anything of him. What did he say?"

"He said, 'Nonsense!'"

Lavina's response was all that he could have hoped. She stared as though her eyes would pop out of her head, and whispered,

*"He said 'Nonsense!' to the Queen?"*

"He did. He said that nobody had ever considered the Ringwood family royal before, and it was too late to start now."

"Oh my goodness!" Lavina exclaimed, full of admiration. "He really stood up to her. What a brave man!"

"He isn't afraid of the Queen, my dear, and she knows it."

"Even so, to defy the Queen to her face!" Lavina said, deeply moved. "We have misjudged him, Papa."

"We have, indeed, my dear."

"I must thank him, and assure him of my true gratitude."

She turned quickly to go in search of the Marquis, but in the doorway she stopped and looked back.

"Papa, what did he mean about being 'safely out of throwing distance'?"

A look of distinct unease passed over the Earl's face.

"Well, my dear – "

"Papa!"

"You have to understand that his first aim was to protect you – "

*"Papa!"*

The Earl sighed and abandoned himself to his fate.

"He said that there was no question of your attending the reception tomorrow, because, as your fiancé, he would not permit you to do so."

"Permit?"

"Well my dear," said the Earl, wishing he could die, "when a woman becomes engaged to a man, it is understood that he assumes a certain authority – "

"*Permit?*"

The Earl gulped.

"That man talked about what he would and would not allow me to do?" she demanded, outraged.

"Only to save us, my dear, by diverting the Queen's wrath to himself. He said that it would not be proper for you to attend a reception to which he was not invited, and that he positively refused you his permission to do so. Lavina, where are you going?"

"To commit murder," she flung over her shoulder.

Her inquiry after the Marquis from a passing servant produced the information that he had gone to the stables. Lavina hurried on, but while she was still some distance she saw him galloping in the direction of the hills.

She ran on to the stables.

"I need your fastest horse," she told the astonished hands.

"His Lordship just took the fastest," a groom told her.

"The next fastest then. Hurry."

In minutes they had brought out a lively animal and struggled to put a side saddle on his back, while he danced about disobligingly, snorting fire.

Lavina knew just how he felt.

At last she leapt onto his back and galloped off into the distance, headed the way she had seen the Marquis go.

After going for a few miles at full speed she saw him, far ahead. He slowed and stopped, then looked back at her, before continuing. She urged her mount to even greater speed until at last she was galloping beside him.

Neck and neck, mile after mile, until at last the horses

slowed from weariness. The Marquis pointed to a stream ahead.

"Our animals have certainly earned the chance to drink," he said. "Let us see to their needs first, then you can tell me what you think of me."

She agreed, and only when the beasts had dipped their heads thankfully into the cool, running water did she allow herself to say,

"When you said you were getting out of throwing distance, I didn't think you'd go to these lengths," Lavina said.

"Well, I knew you would be unreasonably angry."

"Unreasonably? How dare you talk about what you will allow me to do, as though I were a child."

"Not a child, an engaged woman with a sense of propriety."

"But you know that isn't really true," she said furiously.

"Not true that you have a sense of propriety? I hope, for both our sakes, that you are mistaken."

"I mean that I am not an engaged woman."

"For the moment, you are. That gives me certain rights over your behaviour, some of which I am certain that you know about. You're an heiress, aren't you? Your mother left you a great fortune."

"How did you – "

"You surely don't imagine I consented to an engagement without first ascertaining your wealth."

"You didn't have time," she retorted swiftly.

"True, but the wealth of every heiress is known throughout the London clubs. I believe there are even places where fortune hunters can obtain lists, for a fee."

"And are you a fortune hunter, sir?"

"No, luckily I can afford not to be, but that is not true of all men. Picture the poor fellow's dismay if he proposed for your money and found you'd dissipated it before the wedding. So, to protect him, the law says that his fiancée may not dispose of her wealth without his permission.

"Don't breathe fire at me, I am merely giving you an illustration. Your behaviour is very much my concern, and, as I have always made plain, I intend to exercise my authority over you."

"How many times must I say that you do not have any authority over me?"

"You may say it as often as you like. It remains the case that I do. I warned you at the start that I expect you to behave with propriety."

"Are you saying that I do not?"

"I am, indeed. No lady of delicacy would be alone with a man in this isolated spot. If I should insult you with my advances there is nobody to help you."

"I rely on you, as a gentleman, *not* to insult me with your advances."

"But how if your reliance is mistaken?"

Lord Elswick's eyes were glinting strangely.

"Suppose I force my unwelcome attentions on you?" he asked.

For a moment Lavina found it hard to speak. Something seemed to be fluttering in her throat, and her heart was beginning to thump erratically.

"Since we are engaged," she managed to say with spirit, "the presumption would seem to be that your attentions are not unwelcome."

"Do you mean that you pursued me here in the hope of receiving them? Fie on you!"

"I – that is not what I meant – "

Suddenly he was standing very close to her.

"Didn't it occur to you that you were doing something dangerous in coming here alone with me?"

She took a shuddering breath. She would have moved backwards but she found she was standing against a tree.

"I – do not feel – in danger – " she stammered.

"How foolish of you," he said as he lowered his mouth to hers.

There was no escape, even if she were sure she wanted to. His arms were about her body, drawing her hard against him, while his lips caressed hers with ruthless purpose.

At first shock held her still. Then she made a sound of protest and tried to push him away, but he immediately tightened his arms. Anger began to flow through her veins like fire.

But suddenly it was a different fire, made not of anger but of excitement. If she had given in to it she would have strained against him, seeking more kisses and yet more. But pride would not let her do so. She was still angry with him, and if she yielded an inch it would be a victory to him in the battle between them, that had raged since the moment she had burst into his house.

He was proud, but so was she, and she would not let him think he had won her over in the slightest way. She could not afford to.

He seemed to sense her rebellion and began to move his lips more seductively over hers, as though determined to be the winner in this battle.

Lavina's head spun. Suddenly she no longer wanted to fight, but to yield, to give herself to him utterly and completely. Somehow her arms had found their way about his neck and she was pulling his head down to hers, kissing him back eagerly, feverishly.

"Lavina – " he murmured.

His voice seemed to call her back from a great distance. His mouth had released hers, he was looking down into her face with a look of stunned astonishment.

Her breath came raggedly, and suddenly she was herself again, shocked at her own behaviour. How could she have behaved so disgracefully, with such unladylike abandon? He had said that she had no sense of propriety, and she had proved him right.

She pulled away, and this time he released her. She walked a few steps away and stood there, breathing hard.

# CHAPTER SEVEN

After a moment he came close, but did not try to touch her. It seemed a long time before he spoke.

"Forgive me. It is I who lack propriety. I should not have taken advantage of – that is – you are very foolish to be angry with me for – for what I said to the Queen."

"Am I?" she asked in a muffled voice.

"It is well known that Her Majesty believes in the subjection of women – "

Lavina turned and gave him an incredulous stare.

"As long as it's other women," the Marquis added wryly. "She has been known to speak about the 'dreadful wickedness of Women's Rights'. She deludes herself, of course, but she thinks this is what she believes. So I simply used the one argument that she could not answer. Can't you understand that?"

"I suppose so," she said reluctantly.

"I know that, for you, it goes against the grain to defer to me, but in that lies your safety, and your father's safety. It puts the whole responsibility for defying the Queen on to my shoulders, and I promise you I can fight the battle better than either of you."

"You are right, of course," she admitted reluctantly.

"I am doing this as much for your father as for you. His place at court means a lot to him, and if he offends the

Queen too much, he may lose it.

"For your sake, he will take that risk, but he dreads a life without his occupation. If I can get the royal wrath directed at me, he may escape the worst."

"How kind you are," she said impulsively, forgetting how angry she had recently been with him..

"Nonsense," he said, with a return to the brusqueness that was more normal with him.

"But you are, to have thought of him, and how badly he would be hurt. That isn't only kind, it's imaginative."

"You are making a fuss about nothing," he said coldly. "It is merely the most efficient way of managing things. The Queen's wrath means nothing to me because I wouldn't have a place at court for anything she could offer.

"With your father, it's different. He's a convivial man. He likes people, enjoys having them around him. With me, it is different. So don't start attributing sentimental motives to me. Kindness has nothing to do with it."

Lavina looked at him with a touch of sadness.

"I don't believe you," she said at last.

"Then you should know better," he said flatly.

"Why do you hide your better self from people? Would it be so terrible if the world knew you have a side that is generous and sensitive?"

"You were wiser when we first met," he declared. "Then you were hostile to me. You tried to hide it because you were asking my help, but your dislike was there. You should have remained hostile, and I advise you to do so."

"Nonsense!" she said loudly.

He stared.

"What did you say?"

"I said 'nonsense'. If you can say it, so can I. I never heard a man talking such gibberish in all my life."

Her lips curved in an ironical, almost teasing smile.

"So you advise me to stay hostile to you? After the way you just kissed me? Was that designed to make me feel hostile."

She had him there, she was glad to see. He coloured and for a moment his composure deserted him.

"You have a very sharp tongue," he said at last.

"Not sharp," she said, shaking her head. "Swift. Like my perceptions."

"And what – exactly – do you think you perceive?"

She gave him the same smile.

"I'll tell you that another time."

"Yes, let us return," he said with an effort. "We have both talked more than enough nonsense."

\*

For the reception at Balmoral Lavina's appearance was a triumph of Mrs Banty's art. Her gown, with a bustle and a long train was made of cream silk with a matching over-skirt of silk gauze, and a deep flounce of lace.

As the crowning touch she wore the Elswick emeralds which the Marquis, once more using the wonderful modern telegraph system, instructed Hunsbury to bring north.

"I would have brought them with me if I had anticipated this situation," he told Lavina, "but I must confess the Queen's wits were more devious than mine on this occasion. But I think I've made up for it by the other item Hunsbury will be bringing with him."

It turned out to be an exquisite diamond engagement ring, which his mother had previously worn.

Now she was trumpeting to the world that she was unavailable to Prince Stanislaus.

"And by the way," the Marquis added, "The Prince is rather on the short side."

"You know him?" she asked quickly.

"I have encountered him during the course of my travels," the Marquis said coolly. "It hasn't left me eager to know him better. My point was that ladies who wish to earn his goodwill always wear their lowest heels.

"Then I shall wear my highest," Lavina said defiantly.

The Marquis grinned his approval.

The McEwuans felt no resentment at not being included in the invitation. They had never been part of court circles. They cheered the other three on their way with genuine, kindly enthusiasm.

By royal decree, 'tartan would be worn' by those entitled to wear it. Lord Ringwood had borrowed his cousin's kilt, somewhat reluctantly since he lacked the tall, elegant figure necessary to do it justice. But, as he explained to his daughter with a sigh,

"If Her Majesty insists that I show my knobbly knees, then I don't mind doing so in order to placate her."

"Papa, I think you're absolutely heroic," Lavina exclaimed.

If her father lacked the figure to wear a kilt, the same could not be said of the Marquis. He appeared in the kilt of the McDonald clan, explaining that one of his aunts had married the Laird.

"When my valet knew that I was coming to Scotland he insisted on packing it as a precaution," he explained.

He had the long, straight legs necessary to show the kilt as its best, and the broad-shouldered height needed by the black velvet jacket. For once his hair was brushed into a fashionable style.

It was a pity, Lavina thought, that he did not go into society more often, for he was handsome enough to turn all heads.

It was about five miles to Balmoral, and as they drove

through the countryside the day was turning to a soft, enchanting twilight.

Lavina knew that she looked her best in the gorgeous dress, and the emeralds, and at any other time she would have enjoyed the prospect. But tonight she could think only that the Queen was very determined to trap her, and her only safety lay in the Marquis, sitting opposite her.

At this moment he looked capable of dealing with anything. He had an air of lofty grandeur that suited his rank.

He was looking away, regarding the scenery, so that she could see his profile, the slightly hooked nose emphasising the power of his face.

Then he turned to smile at her, and suddenly the world was different. There was unexpected charm in that smile, and for a moment this was the man she had met that night on the boat, when they had entered the world of music together, and found each other.

Then the carriage was slowing down, coming to a halt at Balmoral Castle. Footmen were coming forward to let down the steps and open the doors.

The inside of Balmoral came as a shock. Queen Victoria loved everything Scottish, including the tartans. So there was tartan everywhere in the castle, tartan drapes, tartan furniture coverings, mile after mile of tartan carpet.

Even more astonishing were the 'No Smoking' signs that appeared everywhere. Queen Victoria hated smoking and made it as hard as possible for smokers within her palaces.

Then they were at the entrance to the grand reception room. Lavina and her father were to enter first, with the Marquis behind them.

The Chamberlain cried,

"Lord Ringwood, Lady Lavina Ringwood and Lord Elswick."

She looked down the long carpet at the tiny figure of the Queen at the far end. She was a short woman, but to Lavina she seemed monumental, towering over the whole world, threatening her with a dire fate.

Then she felt a hand reaching for hers, grasping it in a firm, reassuring hold. It was the Marquis, reminding her that he had promised to protect her, no matter what.

She squeezed his hand in return, telling him that she trusted him. Then she stepped forward and began the journey, getting closer to Queen Victoria, and also closer to another figure standing beside her.

It was a man of just under medium height. He had jet black, oily-looking hair and a huge moustache to match. But what really caught Lavina's appalled attention was thick, fat lips, small piggy eyes and an expression of leering self-satisfaction.

This was Prince Stanislaus of Kadradtz, the man that Her Majesty was determined she should marry, no matter what the consequences. She might break her heart or be driven to despair, but by hook or by crook that determined little woman would force her into this hellish marriage.

Lord Ringwood bowed to his sovereign, and Lavina dropped a low, sweeping curtsey.

The Queen remained silent for a long moment, while her face registered cool disdain. When she spoke, her voice was stern.

"How nice to see you, Lord Ringwood – at last! We were very disappointed that you did not see fit to obey our earlier summons on *a matter of national importance*."

The way the Queen said the last words froze Lavina's blood. It told her that Her Majesty was not going to give up without a fight.

"Forgive me, Your Majesty," Lord Ringwood said. "I meant no disrespect, but I was beside myself with joy, celebrating the engagement of my daughter to the Marquis of Elswick, and I'm afraid I got into a muddle."

At the mention of the engagement the Queen's face stiffened, but all she said was,

"It is no matter. Fortunately we are in time to retrieve the situation."

"Good evening, Your Majesty."

The voice was Lord Elswick's, and it was a breach of protocol for him to address the Queen before she had taken notice of him. Lavina saw courtiers stiffen all around them, astonished and outraged at his daring.

But the Marquis knew the game the Queen was playing, and was not going to let her get away with it. Having forced himself to her attention he looked her directly in the eye.

She did not meet his gaze, but directed Lavina and her Papa to the little man standing beside her.

"Price Stanislaus, allow me to present *two members of my family*, the Earl of Ringwood, and his daughter, Lady Lavina Ringwood, of whom you have heard me speak."

There was no mistaking her meaning, or the significant glance the Prince gave to Lavina. His eyes were narrowed in calculation, and yet he seemed to look her over in a moment. A dead smile appeared on his lips.

Lavina shuddered.

As she curtsied in front of him she tried to keep her head up higher than she would normally have done. Her dress was low cut, as was normal with evening gowns, and she was sure this slug-like creature would peer more closely at her *décolletage* than was decent.

As she rose the Prince smiled at her.

"Charming," he said in a heavy accent. "Delightful. You are just as I was led to expect."

Lavina kept her face a determined blank.

"There is surely no reason for Your Royal Highness to have expected anything from me."

He smiled. A cat, contemplating a pot of cream might have smiled like that.

"There is every reason, and I shall take the greatest delight in explaining it to you."

If only, she thought, Papa could help her, but the Queen had detained him in conversation. She was smiling, giving every appearance of friendliness, but Lavina suspected this was a ruse to leave her with Prince Stanislaus.

But there were several other people waiting to be announced, and even the Queen could not hold up the line any longer.

Lord Ringwood moved on to Stanislaus, and greeted him with such an angry glare that Lavina was startled. She had not known that her gentle father was capable of such ferocity.

Stanislaus seemed unperturbed.

"Lord Ringwood, I must congratulate you on your charming daughter. You may consider me an expert. In Kadradtz we know how to appreciate a beautiful woman."

Lord Ringwood's bosom swelled at this vulgar reference to his daughter. As always where his darling was concerned, he rose to new heights.

"Your Royal Highness does my daughter, and myself, too much honour," he said, bowing low.

Stanislaus opened his mouth to speak but the Earl continued,

"I know I speak for Lady Lavina as well as myself when I say that we are deeply honoured at the opportunity of meeting a man whose name rings around the world."

Stanislaus tried again.

"We have heard much of the glories of Kadradtz," Lord Ringwood persisted, raising his voice slightly. "And to meet Your Royal Highness on this occasion only adds to the joy that my family was already feeling on celebrating the betrothal of my daughter, Lavina, to Lord Elswick, whom, as you can see, is here with us."

He stopped because he had run out of breath.

Lavina turned a glance of pure admiration on her father.

Stanislaus' smile had died, replaced by a look of pure malevolence, and his eyes were dead. Quite dead.

"Quite so," he said in a voice like an arctic wind. "Quite so."

Abruptly he turned his head to greet the next guest, but since this was the Marquis he was very little better off.

"Your Royal Highness," the Marquis said.

He gave the smallest bow possible. Then he raised his head and looked the Prince straight in the eye.

All at once Lavina had a terrible sensation. It was as though an earthquake had rocked the hall, shaking the building to its foundations with a terrible roar. Fire blazed, thunder raged, and the air was jagged with hatred.

Then it was over and she was back in the great hall of Balmoral. Everything was just as before, but the impression of what had happened was so powerful that for a moment she was dizzy.

"Papa," she gasped.

He turned quickly, but Lord Elswick was faster, putting an arm firmly about Lavina's waist and drawing her away from the Prince's orbit.

The line moved on, taking them with it. Mercifully it was impossible for the Prince to follow.

"What happened to you, my dear?" the Earl asked.

"I don't know, Papa. I felt such things – as though there was hatred all around me, and somebody had murder in his heart."

"I expect a lot of people would like to murder that man," her father said wisely.

"You were wonderful, Papa."

"You handled him admirably," the Marquis agreed. "What you sensed in the air was probably him wanting to murder you for not letting him get a word in edgeways."

For the first time Lavina noticed that Lord Elswick was rather pale, and although his words were genial there was a strange nervous tension in his voice.

As he drew her arm protectively through his she was aware that he was trembling. She tried to look into his face to divine the cause, but he looked straight ahead and refused to meet her gaze.

Her relief at escaping Prince Stanislaus was short-lived. As the receiving line reached an end Prince Stanislaus came in search of her.

"I have greatly looked forward to escorting you in to supper," he said, taking her hand. "We have much to talk about."

The Marquis made a movement as if to force him to release Lavina's hand, but she stopped him with a brief shake of her head, and a smile.

She did not want to sit next to Stanislaus, but she told herself that she was no baby to make a fuss. What harm could he do her at a public dinner?

So she allowed Stanislaus to lead her away to the long, elegant supper table, where she was to sit next to him.

She was acutely conscious that all eyes were on her. Everybody here knew what the Queen wanted, and knew, also, how determined she could be in pursuit of her own way.

Lavina supposed that another woman might be honoured at the distinguishing attention from a Prince. He devoted himself to her, hanging on her every word as though his life depended on it.

But she could not feel honoured. Even if this man had not threatened all she held dear, he would have been horrible to her. His flattery was not quite right. It was a performance, and he lacked the skill to make it appear real, so that everything was a travesty.

But what was worse than anything was the fact that, at this distance, her worst fears were confirmed.

Prince Stanislaus did not wash.

He tried to smother the odour of stale sweat with a cologne, but the two intermingled to make a smell that was even worse.

He chattered ceaselessly about his country, while Lavina tried to stay out of range of his foul breath.

He told her how delighted she would be with Kadradtz, how she would admire the palace, how the people would love her, and she would love them.

"And the Russians massed on your border?" she enquired sweetly. "Shall I be expected to love them too?"

He was also stupid, for he laughed merrily.

"What Russians? Where do you hear such stories? There are no Russians on the border."

Unfortunately for him there was a lull in the talk at that moment, so that his voice carried all along the table.

The lull turned to shocked silence. All eyes turned from Stanislaus to the Queen, who was looking daggers at her guest of honour.

Lavina took advantage of the silence to say sweetly,

"I am delighted to hear Your Royal Highness say so. I shall know now that we do not need to feel any concern for you."

Stanislaus' eyes became glassy and he realised that he had made a *faux pas*.

The silence seemed to stretch on, with nobody quite knowing how to end it.

The Queen spoke.

"Prince Stanislaus made a most witty observation the other day – "

She repeated the 'witty observation', a dire piece of drivel which fell among the company like a piece of lead. Nonetheless, everyone roared with laughter.

In the relief, Lavina met her father's eye, and saw him wink at her. Then her searching eyes found the Marquis. He was regarding her with a curious little smile, and shook his head as if to say, "Well done!"

So far, so good, Lavina thought. Surely she could get through the rest of the evening?

But worse was to come. As soon as supper was over the Queen announced 'an impromptu dance'. Footmen then made a great play of rolling back carpets, and a pianist sat down at the piano.

"She does this sometimes at Windsor," the Earl groaned. "We're all supposed to think how wonderful and spontaneous it is, and everybody hates it."

"And it's so artificial," Lavina protested. "'Impromptu' indeed!"

"You're not going to escape lightly, I'm afraid," the Earl sighed.

"Well, at least it will give me the chance to make myself plain to Her Majesty," Lavina seethed.

So when the Queen summoned her to sit beside her on the dais, Lavina marched up to her seat, her face set and determined.

"You know why I have sent for you," declared the Queen.

"Yes, ma'am, I do. You wish me to marry Prince Stanislaus, but I regret I am unable to oblige, being already betrothed."

"Nonsense!" The single word dropped from the

Queen's lips like a drop of ice.

"You will do your duty," she declared.

"But what duty?" Lavina asked. "You yourself heard Prince Stanislaus say that he no longer feared the Russians."

Queen Victoria made a noise of contempt.

"The man is a fool," she declared.

"Then how can you want me to marry him?"

"Because it has nothing to do with the matter. Were he ten times a fool, which – between ourselves, I sometimes think he is – your duty would still be plain."

"I intend to do my duty," Lavina returned, "my duty to Lord Elswick, my promised husband."

The Queen's eyes flashed fire. She was not used to being defied.

"We all have to make sacrifices," she said. "I have had to make many sacrifices in my life."

"But you married the man you loved," Lavina pointed out.

For a moment the Queen's face softened.

"That is true," she murmured. "I was more fortunate than you."

"No ma'am," Lavina said firmly. "I intend to be just as fortunate."

For a moment the anger faded from the Queen's face.

"You love him?" she asked. "Lord Elswick? Tell me the truth."

For a moment Lavina hesitated, then she told the truth.

"Yes ma'am. I love him."

"As a wife loves the man at whose side she wishes to pass her life?"

"Yes, ma'am."

"Have you any idea of the closeness of marriage?"

Lavina blushed.

"Yes, ma'am."

"And you wish to share that closeness with this man?"

"Yes, ma'am."

Inwardly Lavina was rejoicing, for surely now the Queen would relent.

The next moment her hopes were cruelly dashed as Victoria said,

"Then I pity you, for your duty is clear. I have promised Prince Stanislaus that you will marry him, and my promise must be kept."

Lavina gasped with outrage.

"You promised him without a word to me? You had no right."

"Young woman, remember to whom you are speaking. As sovereign, I had every right."

"You had no right at all to promise me to a man who doesn't wash. How would you like it?"

"I should not have liked it at all, but if it had been my duty, I should unhesitatingly have done so."

"Then Your Majesty is made of sterner stuff than I. I will not do it."

"You will do as I say!"

"No, ma'am, I will not."

The Queen regarded her in sulphurous silence.

The Marquis appeared at the foot of the dais, bowing to his monarch, and saying,

"Forgive me, ma'am, for being a too possessive fiancé, but as Lady Lavina is my future wife, I do not like to be apart from her for long."

"You will have to bear yourself in patience a little longer," the Queen declared coldly. "Prince Stanislaus is my guest of honour, and I have promised him an opportunity to dance with Lady Lavina."

"Certainly," Lavina said, rising to her feet. "That will give me another chance to make my position plain to him."

She descended to the foot of the dais, turning to curtsey to the furious Queen. Etiquette demanded that she wait until Her Majesty gave her permission to depart, but having gone so far she felt brave enough for anything. Queen Victoria could hardly be angrier with her than she was already.

Prince Stanislaus was bearing down on her, his arms opened to seize her.

"Are you all right?" the Marquis asked.

"Yes, thank you," she said crisply. "I think I shall manage this very well."

She had defeated a Queen. In her present mood, a Prince would present no problem.

# CHAPTER EIGHT

Lavina faced Prince Stanislaus with her head up, allowing him to fit his arms about her and take her onto the dance floor.

She moved correctly, but stiffly, holding herself like a ramrod, until he complained.

"You might be a little more accommodating."

"I am doing my duty Your Royal Highness."

"Well, it's a very bleak business if that's all you're doing," he snapped.

"My duty is all I am required to do," she informed him coolly.

Stanislaus grimaced, but said no more for a few moments. Meanwhile, as he danced, he tried to hold her closer and closer, efforts which were largely defeated by her stiffness.

"Now, come along, this will never do," he said at last in a wheedling tone. "You really must make some effort to get along with me. I'm very willing to get along with you. I think you're pretty and charming, and will grace the throne of Kadradtz."

When she set her mouth and stubbornly refused to answer, he persisted,

"It is the Queen's wish, and you must obey your Queen, you know."

"Does everybody obey you in your country?" she asked.

"Certainly they do, otherwise I devise horrible tortures for them."

"What a delightful place!"

"It is the most delightful place in the world," he agreed, too stupid to detect her irony. "You will love it."

"I will not love it, for I will never see it. In fact I wish never to see you again."

"Since we are to be married, that will hardly be possible," he said, smiling.

"I am not going to marry you. I have just told Her Majesty so."

"And she has told me that you are."

"I think my fiancé might have something to say about that," she said, emboldened by the discovery that the Marquis had them under observation the whole time, frequently moving his position so that he never lost sight of her.

"Oh, be hanged to him!" Stanislaus said impatiently. "I'm tired of all this rubbish about fiancés. It's time we had a private talk."

They were near a large set of French windows that opened onto a broad terrace. Suddenly Stanislaus' tightened his grip and began whirling her in the direction of the open windows.

Lavina tried to resist but he was too strong for her. She could feel everything slipping out of her control, and her fear began to rise.

But then Stanislaus came to an abrupt halt, uttering a violent curse.

"Get out of my way," he snapped.

"No," said the Marquis, standing, immobile, in the window.

"I said get out of my way."

The Marquis spoke so quietly that only the three of them could hear.

"You deserve to be knocked senseless, and if you do not release her at once, I will do it myself."

He leaned closer, and spoke more quietly still, in a voice of such cold menace that Lavina was startled.

"You don't really doubt me, do you? You know damned well that I'll do it. Now release her before you feel my fist."

It would be too much to say that Stanislaus released Lavina, but he was so stunned that he froze, and she was able to slip from his grasp.

The Marquis took advantage of the moment to put his arm firmly around her waist.

"You are looking pale, my love," he said, in a voice loud enough to be heard. "I feel sure you are affected by the heat."

"Yes – yes – " she gasped, playing up to him by putting her hand to her head and swaying.

Half guiding, half carrying her the Marquis made his way over to the Queen, followed by Lord Ringwood, who had seen everything.

"Your Majesty," he said smoothly, "my fiancée is feeling unwell and, with your gracious permission, we will depart before she is quite overcome."

The Queen's face was sour with temper and she looked as though she would give anything to refuse permission. But there was nothing she could do. She gave a curt nod.

Instantly the Marquis swept Lavina up in his arms and marched out of the hall, followed by the Earl.

Lavina clung to him. She was not fainting, but she had her wits sufficiently about her to assume a swooning position, at least until they were safely in the carriage.

"Lavina," he said.

She realised that she was still clinging to him tightly, her eyes closed.

She opened them, and found him looking directly into her face with a serious, troubled expression.

"Lavina," he said again. "Are you all right?"

"Yes," she said, disengaging herself and feeling glad that the darkness hid her blushes.

He released her and she sank back against the upholstery.

"I'm so glad that's over," she said. "I couldn't have endured him another moment. Thank you, thank you for coming to my rescue. I'm afraid it will have made the Queen very angry with you."

The Marquis' only response to this was a shrug.

"I, too, am overwhelmed with gratitude – " the Earl began to say, but Lord Elswick interrupted him, almost rudely.

"My dear sir, think nothing of it."

"But – "

"I would be grateful if you would say no more."

The Marquis sounded almost angry.

For the rest of the journey he did not speak, but sat, isolated in the far corner of the carriage, staring out of the window into the darkness.

Lavina would have liked to reach out to him, and beg him to share his feelings with her, but he seemed to have withdrawn into a far place, where he would not allow her to follow.

Later that night, lying in her bed, she recalled other aspects of the evening.

When she thought of the conversation between herself

and the Queen she could only be thankful that she was alone, with darkness to cover her burning cheeks.

She had said bluntly that she loved Lord Elswick.

She had spoken in a temper, but now, forced to be honest with herself, she knew that it was true.

She had given her love to a man who did not love her. He had kissed her, but more out of anger than passion. And he had never given her any reason to believe that he was moved by tender emotions towards her.

He was saving her, yet he was doing so for some reason that she did not understand, and which he would not confide in her.

And yet she loved him. And when the Queen had asked her if she understood about the closeness of marriage she had thought of Lord Elswick with passion.

It shamed her to think of it now. How could she feel such things for a man who felt nothing for her?

Or did he?

She remembered the way his lips had scorched hers, the trembling she had felt in his body as they embraced.

Might she not build a little hope on that?

At last she got out of bed and went restlessly to the window, looking out onto the moonlit scenery. In the brilliant pale blue light the mysterious hills stretched far away.

Here in Scotland she had seen aspects of the Marquis that she might otherwise never have known. She had seen him tender with music, and tonight, murderous with rage.

She knew she would have been afraid if he had turned that black countenance on her. And Stanislaus had been afraid. He had met his match, and he knew it.

"And so have I," she thought. "I too have met my match."

Then a memory came back to her, of something her father had said when she had just started her first season, and was already a brilliant success.

Young man had thronged round her, some simply flirting, but others with their hearts in their eyes. But her father had said,

"Don't take them too seriously, my darling, or be in a rush to marry. Remember you will be marrying for life. Not just for a few weeks in the country enjoying the tennis and the swimming, but for life!"

"I don't suppose the men I meet for the first time are likely to propose to me," Lavina had said.

"It's is only a question of time before a man lays his heart at your feet and asks you to become his wife."

"That will be exciting," Lavina had murmured.

"Very exciting for the moment," her father had replied. "But you have to remember that he must be a man who will be more important than anyone else, and eventually be the father of your children."

He had stopped speaking, and then his voice deepened as he went on,

"However difficult your life will be, you will be his completely and absolutely, for all time. That is why it's important that you do not make up your mind too quickly."

Lavina remembered saying lightly,

"But I'm happy with you, Papa. It's so exciting being in London that I don't want to worry about marrying anyone and leaving home."

"But one day you will want to, when the right man appears and makes you forget everything else. I simply want you to understand that you will be changing your life, not just for a few minutes, like a dance, or as one might say, a visit to the moon, but for eternity."

There was a pause before he added,

"When you marry I want you to marry a man you love and who loves you. Just as your own happiness will rest on his heart, so he will find you the most perfect, the most adorable and the most wonderful woman he has ever met. Only if you both feel like that can you have the happiness which your Mother and I found together."

Lavina had never forgotten that. It came back to her now as she stood in the moonlit window, and thought of the man who had made her forget everything else.

"He certainly doesn't think me perfect, adorable and wonderful, as Papa says," she thought.

"In fact, he isn't really the right man at all," she added, almost crossly. "He's the wrong man in every possible way. So why is it that I can't help loving him? Why does he make me forget all the pleasant, charming men, and think only of him? *Why?*"

But the cold moon had no answer for her.

*

The next day, Lord Elswick continued in the same, tense manner as the evening before. Sometimes when he looked at Lavina she thought she detected almost a kind of savagery in his eyes.

Yet he refused to leave her side, even turning down the chance to go fishing to linger in the conservatory while the ladies sewed.

This astounded Lavina, as she was sure he must feel this was an occupation for bedlam.

"Be careful not to leave the house," he said.

"You don't think – ?"

"I think he'll come calling, yes. And our hostess must deny that you're here."

To Lady McEwuan he spun a pretty tale of how the

117

Prince's ardour had overcome his manners the night before. She was enchanted, and easily agreed to protect her guest.

Sure enough, Stanislaus arrived half an hour later. Lavina saw him from the window and darted back into the house, encountering the Marquis almost at once.

"He's here."

"Don't worry, Lady McEwuan will tell him that you are resting after the excitements of last night. All you need do, is stay out of sight."

Down below, Lady McEwuan was playing her part with zest. Her delight at greeting a Prince was soon spoiled by his offensive manners, and the smell of pomade that wafted from him.

He stayed for an hour, refusing all hints to leave, until at last he seemed to accept that he was on a useless errand, scowled and departed.

Lavina watched him depart from behind a lace curtain. She shuddered and buried her face in her hands, wondering if she would be pursued all her life, and how long the Marquis would be there to shield her.

"It's all right, he's gone now," came the Marquis' voice.

"Will he ever be gone?" she asked in a muffled voice. "Will I ever be safe from him?"

Now, she thought, a man who cared about her, might say that he would marry her, and keep her safe that way.

But the silence stretched on and on.

At last he spoke.

"We will just have to be more patient than he is. We can prolong this engagement until he gives in."

Something seemed to die inside her. She had lost. He did not want her. Distraught, she kept her hands over her face.

The next moment she felt Lord Elswick turning her towards him, and drawing her hands down. Something he

118

saw made him grow still, watching her with a wondering expression.

In the silence he took one of her hands and turned it over so that he could lay his lips against the palm. His breath scorched Lavina, and a fiery excitement began to travel along her nerves, from her head down to her heart, and from there outwards until it engulfed her whole body.

She gasped with the intensity of the sensations that possessed her more completely than anything she had known in her life.

Yet, although they thrilled her, they also scared her. It was not proper for a young lady to feel such physical delight, not unless she was sure of the man's love, and she was not.

"No," she said, snatching her hand away. "You must not."

"Why must I not?"

"Because it – it isn't right."

"Because you find my touch unpleasant?"

"You know that I do not," she said in a low voice.

"Then why is it not right? We are betrothed. If there is one man whose embraces you may accept, that man is myself. Indeed, I should take the greatest exception if I were to find you in the arms of any other man."

"But we are not really betrothed," she said. "You know that we are not."

He did not answer, and when she looked up she found him regarding her with a grave expression that contained no hint of his usual defensive irony.

"I wonder how all this will end," he said quietly.

Something in his tone made her heart beat faster. For a moment she could not speak. When she finally found her voice it was to say, with more firmness than she felt,

"It will end when that dreadful man gives up. Then I

will thank you for your great kindness, and we shall part friends."

"Friends? Is that what we'll be?"

Again there was that strange vibrant note, warning her that everything he said had a double meaning.

"We shall certainly never be enemies," she said. "Not on my side. How could I ever be your enemy?"

"That was not what I meant, and you know it."

The tingling excitement going all through her told her what he had really meant. How could she ever feel merely friendship for a man who could make her feel like this, in her body and in her heart.

He was hinting at something deeper that flowed between them, yet he seemed reluctant to say it more plainly.

"Then I do not know what you mean," she said, turning her head away.

He reached for her quickly and pulled her round to face him, and for a moment she saw a fierce intensity in his face. His breath was coming feverishly and his eyes were bright.

"Lavina – " he said.

"Yes," she whispered. "Yes – "

At any moment, she was sure, he would tell her of his passion, perhaps of his love. And then all would be well between them. She would be free to acknowledge the intensity of her own feelings without shame.

If only he would speak!

But the silence stretched agonisingly on and on.

She knew what tormented him.

She was a woman, and therefore someone to be distrusted. Even if he loved her, he would still be suspicious of her, even, perhaps, hostile.

And what use was love if it could not overcome

suspicion and hostility, if it were not even strong enough to allow him to speak plainly?

And then he let her go. He stepped back abruptly. No words had been spoken.

"You are right," he said harshly. "I mean nothing. Nothing at all."

He stepped back and gave her a small courteous bow.

"I beg your pardon for troubling you."

\*

Next day there was a sensation. Throughout the district word spread like wildfire that Her Majesty was departing Balmoral.

"She's been there barely a week," Sir Ian said to Lord Ringwood. "She's never been known to go so soon before."

"Perhaps it's a false alarm," said the Earl, not daring to hope too soon.

"No, Her Majesty's carriage was seen journeying to Ballater Station. There was a man with her. He had a big, black moustache."

"The Prince," Lavina said. "He's gone. Oh Papa, I'm safe."

"For the moment," said the Marquis, who had been listening. "I don't think the Queen will give up that easily, but she seems to have realised that trying to bully you up here won't work."

That night there was a large dinner-party, given by Sir James McVein.

The whole family was wearing tartan, the men in kilts, the women in white silk with tartan sashes over one shoulder, fastened at the waist by diamond clips.

"Lord Elswick has sent you this, my dear," Lavina's father said, opening a small box to reveal a large diamond clip.

"There was no need for him to trouble himself, Papa," Lavina said coolly. "Dear Lady McEwuan had loaned me one of hers."

"But surely she would understand if you – "

"I would not be impolite to our hostess for anything in the world," Lavina said, setting her chin in a stubborn way that told her father it was useless for him to continue.

When everyone gathered downstairs she waited for the Marquis to make some comment, but after looking her over he merely said coolly,

"My compliments on your appearance, ma'am."

Lavina wished that she could explain that he had insulted her by coming to the edge of a declaration and then backing off; and that her snubbing of his gift was merely her way of saying that she was hurt that he could not trust her.

But since no such explanation was possible she was forced to keep her feelings to herself. She travelled the short distance to the McVein estate in disgruntled silence.

But it was impossible to remain disgruntled in the merry atmosphere she found when she got there. James had put himself out to entertain his neighbours.

The house was filled with light. The halls were hung with garlands of greenery and berries.

There were nearly a hundred guests, but the family from the castle were the guests of honour, and to James, it was clear, Lavina was the guest of honour.

Since he had invited her riding, and the Marquis had so effectively denied them privacy, he had made no open overtures to her, although he had usually been there at the dinners they had attended.

Now he came forward to greet her, hands outstretched, with a beaming smile.

"There's not a woman here who can hold a candle to you," he said.

"Hush!" she said, putting her finger to her lips and giving him a sparkling smile. "Remember your duty to the other ladies."

His reply was a wink.

"Good evening, McVein."

The Marquis held out his hand to his host, greeted him blandly, then devoted himself to his host's mother.

The dinner table was a masterpiece of flowers and exquisite china, lit by candles. Smiling, James led Lavina to a place beside him.

As they ate a piper walked round the table, playing merry tunes on the bagpipes. Yet Lavina could still manage to hear James' chatter, which consisted mainly of jokes.

They were good jokes and Lavina laughed often. Her host's blatant admiration was like balm to her wounded spirit, and she almost forgot to eat.

The food, however, was delicious, so was the wine. It was a long time since Lavina had enjoyed a party so much.

Then James rose to his feet, raising his full wine glass into the air, and the toast of *Slainte Mhath* could be heard round the room.

It was all great fun and when the ladies left the dining-room, Lavina found herself hoping the men would not stay long.

In fact, they joined them twenty minutes later to usher them into the ballroom, where a pipe band was waiting to play.

Soon it became clear that Lavina was the belle of the ball. All the men wanted to dance with her, and pay her extravagant compliments.

She passed from partner to partner, hearing the praise of all, until at last she found herself waltzing with the Marquis.

"Are you sure you can spare me a dance?" he asked

ironically.

She had to admit to herself that she had avoided him, because she did not wish to feel his arms about her in the waltz, but she was too proud to let him suspect that.

"You've had no shortage of partners," she told him coyly. "Don't expect me to pity you as a wall-flower."

"I do not, but, as I told you once before, I expect you to behave properly."

"And I do not believe I have offended against propriety," she teased. "This is a ball, sir, and even an engaged woman is permitted to flirt a little."

"Not if she is engaged to me," he said firmly.

"But I am not engaged to you," she whispered so that only he could hear.

His face darkened, and she was suddenly aware that this man hated any woman who even hinted at putting him second.

"No, you are not," he said bitingly. "Do you wish me to announce that fact in this company?"

"No," she said swiftly.

"Are you certain? Surely Sir James McVein would be only too glad to have me out of the way."

She could not believe that he was being so unreasonable as to indulge in this violent over-reaction.

Could he not see that she was only flirting with other men because her heart was sore that he had neglected her.

"I have no interest in Sir James," she said, now growing angry in her turn.

"You amaze me, madam, after the way you have lived in his pocket this evening."

"How dare you! I have not lived in his pocket."

"I say you have. I say also that if you make a fool of me again I shall walk out of this house and leave you to your own devices."

"You are behaving abominably."

"Do I have your word that you will respect my wishes?"

"You are being a tyrant – "

"Do I have your word, or do I walk off the floor?"

Lavina pulled herself free.

"Let me save you the trouble," she snapped, and walked away from him.

Unfortunately – or perhaps fortunately – the dance ended at that moment, so few people noticed her gesture, and the effect was lost.

After that she stayed with her father, ready to repel the Marquis if he should approach her.

But he did not approach her, and when they were ready to depart, Lady McEwuan said that Lord Elswick had made his apologies and gone home early.

*

Lord Elswick went out early next morning, so Lavina had no chance to make up with him. Her morning was one of pure misery, until a servant brought her a letter.

Eagerly she opened it. In a large, strong hand, it read,

*Forgive me, and come to me quickly. There is so much I want to say to you, that is only for your ears. Seek out the cottage by the stream that runs through the wood. I'm waiting for you there. Hurry, my beloved.*

*Ivan.*

"Ivan!" She said his name to herself. The Marquis had never asked her to call him by his given name, despite the fact that they were supposed to be engaged.

Yet now he asked her forgiveness, and used his name as a sign of intimacy. He had called her beloved, and chosen a remote spot where nobody would disturb them, because he longed to be alone with her.

Her heart overflowed with joy.

She sped up to her room to change hurriedly into riding clothes, then down again as fast as she could, then to the stables.

In minutes she was on her way, alone. Ivan would not expect her to take a groom this time.

In half an hour she had reached the wood and began to move through it. There was the stream and the cottage, just ahead. And there, just outside the cottage, was a single horse, tied to a tree.

She tied her own horse beside it and pushed open the door.

"Here I am!" she cried. "Here I am, my darling!"

The door slammed behind her.

She whirled round, smiling with the force of her joy.

Then her smile faded, and a look of revulsion took its place.

Standing there, leering at her, was Prince Stanislaus.

# CHAPTER NINE

"You!" she cried with loathing. "What are you doing here?"

"I've hired this cottage. I thought it would make a good place for us to meet. So obliging of you to come in answer to my letter."

"*Your* letter? But – "

She stopped. The hideous truth was becoming clear to her.

"Of course, my letter. How else could I have got you here?"

"You can't have written it," she said, her breath coming in little gasps. "It started, 'Forgive me.' You could never have known that we'd quarrelled."

Stanislaus gave his strange, silent laugh, and it chilled her blood.

"My dear lady, I had no idea that you and Elswick had quarrelled until you told me just now. But if there's one thing I've learned about women in many delightful years spent pursuing them, it is that every woman thinks her lover is in the wrong.

"He can be a saint, it makes no difference. She is always sulky and petulant about something. So a clever man asks her forgiveness as a matter of routine. He can rely on her to supply the details.

"And I was right, you see, because now you are here."

"And I am leaving immediately."

"I'm afraid you are not. Your presence is important to me."

Grasping her riding whip tightly, Lavina took a step forward, facing him and saying firmly,

"Get out of my way."

Stanislaus merely laughed.

"How splendid you are! How magnificent! What a Princess you will make."

"I will never be your Princess!"

"Oh but you will. You have no choice. I must have an English royal bride – "

"I am not royal – "

"The Queen has recognised you as part of her family. When we marry she will consider me a relative, and from that, many good things will flow.

"You see, it's not just protection against the Russians that I need. It's money. When I'm related to the British royal family, money will flow into my coffers."

"For the benefit of your people."

"But what benefits me, benefits my people. Naturally I am expected to maintain a splendid court. As my Princess you will be at the centre of luxury. You will enjoy it."

"You are out of your mind. Even if I married you – which I won't – how could I ever enjoy luxury paid for by stealing from your people? The idea is horrible?"

"Do you think so? I find it rather sensible? How else could I pay for my little pleasures. Your scruples won't last. When I shower you with diamonds, you'll forget to worry about who paid for them."

Lavina shuddered. His leering smile, his soft, lisping voice, was beginning to make her feel sick.

"Get out of my way," she repeated. "I want to leave."

"But you cannot leave. Here you are, and here you will stay."

"Until what? Are you planning to produce a parson to force me into marriage here and now? Because if you – "

"Good heavens no!" he said, genuinely shocked. "No hole in the corner business for us. To be any use to me our wedding must take place in the sight of the world. I need a great occasion, in Westminster Abbey, in the presence of the Queen and the Russian ambassador, with the ceremony conducted by the Archbishop of Canterbury."

"And just how do you think you'll force me to go through with it?" she demanded.

"By keeping you here alone with me until you're so compromised that no other man will have you."

"So you plan to turn me into damaged goods," she said scornfully. "And what use will I be then as Princess of Kadradtz?"

He shrugged.

"Don't be so stupid! It doesn't matter to me if you're damaged goods, as long as you bring the money with you."

A chill went through Lavina as she realised that this creature was right.

Nobody knew where she was.

He could keep her here for days without being discovered.

And who would want her then?

"Her Majesty will never allow you to do this," she said desperately.

"Why not?" he asked, genuinely puzzled.

"When she knows how you kidnapped me – I shall beg her help."

Stanislaus roared with laughter.

"You beg her help? After the way you spoke to her?"

He was right. She had thrown away all chance of the Queen's friendship, and now her position was truly desperate.

Suddenly she turned and began to run, heading for the far door. But she found it locked, and when she turned she saw Stanislaus coming towards her. He did not move hurriedly, for he knew that she was trapped.

"Let me go," she said breathlessly. "I will not marry you."

"Don't be ridiculous," he said, abandoning his smile and showing her a cold face. "Of course you will. I want you. You are necessary to my plans. Forget Elswick. He won't want you when you've spent a few days in my company."

"I am not going to spend any time in your company," she said emphatically. "I am going to leave now."

"How, I wonder?"

"I can't believe that you'll try to keep me here against my will."

"My dear girl, I didn't take all this trouble to get you here simply to let you leave. I need you, I want you, and I always get what I want."

"You won't get me."

Lavina tried to sound firm, but her heart was beating with fear.

"Why, who do you think will help you?"

"My fiancé," she said determinedly. "Lord Elswick, the man I am going to marry."

Prince Stanislaus roared with laughter.

"Marry you? Have you deluded yourself with that idea? He has no intention of marrying you. Your engagement is false, a fantasy for my benefit."

"That is not true," she stammered.

"The Queen tells me that it *is* true. She never expected you to carry the charade this far. She thought, when her wishes had been made clear to you, you would obey them. But since you are stubborn, stern methods are needed."

"Do you expect me to believe that the Queen actually supports you in abducting me? Never!"

"Well, I didn't exactly describe what I meant to do, but in general she supports our coming marriage."

"*I will not marry you*," she screamed.

"When we've been here alone for a few days, you'll be glad to marry me. Elswick won't claim you. Oh, he wants revenge on me, but not at the price of tying himself to damaged goods."

"What – do you mean – revenge?"

"You didn't know? How charming. I shall have the pleasure of telling you. I was the man who enticed his bride away and left him looking foolish at the church, to the derision of his neighbours."

Lavina stared at him, aghast.

"I don't believe you," she whispered.

But she did. It made sense of everything, including the way the Marquis had behaved at their first meeting.

At first he had refused to help her, then her father had mentioned Kadradtz, and he had swung round from the window, alert at the name.

From that moment he had been determined to do everything in his power to make their betrothal convincing. The hastily arranged dinner party, the man from the newspaper, the family jewels, the kiss during the fireworks display – he had done much, much more than she had envisaged when she asked his help.

And this was his reason. It was all to thwart the man who had ruined his life.

She closed her eyes, trying not to follow this path of

thought. It led to too much pain.

"I don't believe you," she said again. It was untrue but she wanted to keep him talking. Dreadful as it was, she had to hear everything.

He shrugged.

"Why not? I don't live in Kadradtz all the time. It's a dreadful, primitive place, as you'll discover when we're married. I travelled extensively, and at that time I was in England. I happened to meet Anjelica.

"She took my fancy. She was a pretty little thing, delightful enough to turn any man's head. When I met her she'd already got to work on young Elswick, thinking she'd struck gold.

"He was insane about her, wildly, desperately infatuated. I think he would have sacrificed the world, and counted it well lost if only he could have her.

"It was the kind of love a man feels only once in a lifetime – or so they tell me. I've never wasted time like that, myself. But people who understand these things say that, afterwards, a man protects himself from ever loving like that again."

"Yes," Lavina whispered. "Oh yes."

"Personally," continued Stanislaus with ineffable smugness, "I think that to be making such a fuss over a woman is absurd. One woman is just like another in the end.

"Some are a little more fun, some a little less, but none of them really matter. However, Elswick would have died for Anjelica."

Lavina looked away, refusing to let him see how these remarks tortured her. They conjured up thoughts she could not bear, thoughts of the man she loved as he had once been, young, generous, with a heart to give; not wary and defensive as he was now, but loving, passionate and giving.

"Anjelica knew how wildly in love he was," Stanislaus

went on. "She thought she was winning. She hadn't reckoned on his family cutting him off.

"Of course they couldn't deprive him of the title, and if she'd been patient, she would eventually have been a Marchioness, and everything would have been hers.

"But Anjelica didn't understand the words 'patience' and 'eventually'. She wanted everything now, and I was able to offer 'now'. Not marriage, of course, but money, jewels, life in glittering surroundings.

"She made me wait right up until the wedding day. She was sure his family would relent when the moment came, and turn up at the wedding.

"She even went to the church, all dressed in bridal white. I went with her, riding beside her carriage. When she realised that the old Marquis wasn't there, I took her hand and we ran away together."

Stanislaus gave his eerie, almost silent laugh.

"At the last minute I looked back and saw the jilted bridegroom standing there. For a moment I'll swear he didn't even realise what was happening. Then he began to run after us, calling her name.

"But we ran and I took her up on my horse in front of me, and off we galloped. He chased us out of the church, still calling her name.

"I heard afterwards that he lay in a fever for weeks, and nearly lost his reason."

"Sweet heaven!" Lavina whispered.

"Oh she was a prime article, I grant you. Everyone envied me for having such a creature on my arm.

"In Kadradtz we understand this kind of relationship better than the prudish English. I was able to take her with me everywhere."

"And you expect me to marry you, knowing that this woman is your mistress?" Lavina demanded scathingly.

"Good heavens, no! I haven't seen her for years. I became bored with her very quickly. Her conversation was extremely limited and her charms soon faded. Besides, another comet streaked across my horizon, far more beautiful and equally avaricious."

"I can see why you would need money," Lavina said bitingly, "with all these jewels to buy."

"Oh please! Credit me with some understanding of economy. Naturally I retrieved the jewels from Anjelica to pass on to her successor. Not that they suited her very well. She was a brunette, and pearls looked insipid on her. Still, one can't have everything."

Lavina stared at him, speechless with disgust.

"So you threw her out without a penny when she'd outlived her usefulness?"

"Not exactly without a penny. I did give her a sum of money. It was the only way to stop her caterwauling, and be rid of her. But I doubt it lasted long.

"My, how that woman could spend! Elswick could never have afforded her. Mind you, if she'd known how soon he would inherit the title, she might have decided to marry him and bide her time."

Now Lavina understood the jagged hatred that had rent the air when Lord Elswick met the Prince at Balmoral. It had not been her imagination. It had been real.

"Still, I think she was very satisfied with me," Stanislaus said smugly, "for a while."

Suddenly Lavina recalled something Lord Elswick had said at Balmoral. It had puzzled her, but it made perfect sense now.

"But he pursued you," she said in a voice of wondering discovery. "He found you and knocked you senseless, just as he threatened to do again that night at Balmoral."

There was a note in her voice that was almost triumph.

"You've felt his fist before, haven't you? That was what he meant when he said you knew he'd do it."

A pained looked passed over Stanislaus' face.

"There was an undignified brawl, I admit. In Heidelberg, not Kadradtz, which was a pity. In my own country I could have locked him up for ever, but in Heidelberg it had to be left to the officers of the law.

"One of them turned out to be an old drinking companion of his father, and got him out of the country, fast. I was very annoyed about that."

Lavina managed a brave laugh.

"I wish I could have seen you when he'd thrashed you. You must have been a sight."

"You are really most unwise to speak to me like that you know."

"I shall speak as I like. I care nothing for you. I shall never marry you."

"You're not cherishing hopes of marrying Elswick, are you? Oh dear, I do hope he hasn't deluded you into thinking he cares for you. He's quite capable of it, simply to keep you compliant."

Lavina refused to let her face reveal her inner torment.

Was that all his kisses had meant – to ensure that she played her part properly? His anger when she had ventured on a mild flirtation – was that simply to ensure that she did not make a fool of him?

"Anyway," Stanislaus continued, "I'm sure you're beginning to understand the reality of the situation now. You've been used. Ivan Elswick wanted to revenge himself on me, and you were his tool. Once he knows he's lost the battle he won't have any further use for you."

Lavina drew in a sharp breath. It was all true, and it hurt unbearably.

Then she realised that Stanislaus was walking towards

her, with a significant leer.

"So why don't you try to be a little accommodating? After all, we're going to be here together for quite a while."

He reached for her and she drew back her riding whip to strike him, but he grabbed her hand.

For a moment they struggled. She was desperate, but he was stronger, and she could feel that in another moment he would overcome her.

And then she heard an incredible sound.

The click of a pistol being cocked.

Followed a voice of iron,

"You have one second to release her, or I swear I'll pull the trigger and damn the consequences."

Twisting her head, Lavina nearly gave a cry of joy.

It was Lord Elswick, holding a pistol to the Prince's head.

"You are being very unwise," Stanislaus began.

"*One second.*"

The Prince released her. Lavina got as far away from him as possible.

"Thank God!" she gasped.

"There's no time for that now," he grated, glancing at her briefly.

"*Ivan, look out!*"

With a movement that was incredibly lithe, considering his figure, Stanislaus had wriggled free and whipped out a knife.

With an oath the Marquis turned the pistol so that he was holding the barrel, and brought the butt down on Stanislaus' head.

He fell to the floor and lay there groaning, blood pouring down his face.

"He's all right," the Marquis said, seizing Lavina's

hand. "Let's go."

She needed no telling twice, running with him as fast as she could, then outside. There she found a downpour, with the rain coming down so hard that for a moment Lavina was driven back.

"On your horse," Lord Elswick said, helping her to mount. "And ride as fast as you can."

All she wanted was to get away from here and then to be alone with him, to look into his eyes and see the truth. But she knew that would have to wait.

At first the trees protected them from the heavy rain, but gradually the wood faded, they were out in the open and the full force of the storm hit them. Rain came down in sheets, alarming the horses and making it hard to see the road ahead.

"We shall have to find some shelter until the worst has passed," he said. "I think I passed an inn half a mile along here."

They reached the inn, soaked and weary, and were relieved to find that it was open and they could get under cover.

"The lady needs a private parlour," the Marquis said at once.

The landlord bowed her into a small parlour at the back, and instructed a maid to take in some towels.

When Lavina had finished drying her hair she found that the Marquis had joined her. He pulled off his sodden coat and dried himself off as best he could.

His damp shirt still stuck to him, his hair was tousled, and he was breathing hard, almost as though he were still fighting.

The sight made Lavina remember what Stanislaus had said. For the Marquis this was a battle that had already lasted a long time, and it wasn't over yet.

"Lavina – "

He reached for her, pulling her close, wrapping his arms about her. For a moment her soul rejoiced, but only for a moment. His caresses were poisoned for her now.

Instead of melting against him, as she longed to do, she stiffened and asked in a hard voice,

"How did you find me?"

"You dropped the letter in your room and your maid found it. I guessed who had sent it, and luckily it told me where you'd gone."

She wanted to cry out at the thought that he had seen that letter and believed it was from him.

She was grateful for being rescued, but her spirit was still wretched from what she had discovered. Suddenly she could hardly bear to be with him.

She pulled back, turning away from him.

"My dearest – " he reached for her again.

"Don't," she cried, backing from him. "Don't call me that. Don't come near me."

"But what is it? Are you angry with me? Did you think I wouldn't come for you?"

"Oh to be sure, you had to play out your revenge to the end?" she cried.

"Darling – "

"*You should have told me.*"

His face hardened.

"So Stanislaus has been talking. I dare say he made a good story of it."

"I wish you had told me yourself. I felt so foolish to learn the truth from him."

"How could I tell you?" he demanded harshly. "You asked for my help and I gave it. I could not speak of my reasons to you then. They were too painful. And why should

I think you cared, as long as I did as you asked?"

She took a deep breath.

"Yes of course. You are right." She tried to force herself to speak sensibly. "I am very grateful for everything you have done for me, and now that it's over I – "

"Is it over?"

"It must surely be over very soon. The Prince will not stay here now. He will retire defeated, and then you will have everything you wanted."

"Not quite everything," he murmured.

Lavina did not hear him. She was walking around the room, trying to sound composed, hoping desperately that he would not guess she was actually tortured by anguish.

"You made use of me," she cried.

"In the beginning – yes, but that was before we knew each other. Have you not felt what has happened between us? Do I need to say in words that I have fallen in love with you – deeply in love, as I never thought to be again?"

They were the words she had longed to hear, but now they seemed to have no meaning. In her distraught state nothing reached her clearly.

Nothing in the world was real, or as it should be. She had fallen into another dimension, the one shown her by Stanislaus, a place of deceit and misery.

It was like tumbling into the pit of hell, and even a declaration of love from the man she adored reached her sounding like mockery from a grinning devil.

"Lavina, let us put the past behind us and start again," he implored. "Let me hear you say that you love me."

"No," she cried hoarsely, "no, get away from me. There can never be anything between us."

He stopped and a strange withered look crossed his face.

"Are you saying that you do not love me? That I have been living in a sweet delusion."

"Yes," she cried, "and so have I. There is nothing in the world but delusion and lies."

She barely knew what she was saying or doing, but somehow she had opened the far door of the room. It led into a passage, and she flew down that passage as though escaping demons.

She wrenched open the back door and fled outside. The wind and rain had dropped now and she ran across the yard, through the back gate, out into the countryside.

She did not know where she was going. She only knew that she had to get away from him. She could hear his voice crying her name, but she only ran harder.

Suddenly the world was filled with a terrifying sound, like an explosion.

In the same moment she saw a flash of light just up ahead.

She stopped, not realising what had happened. Her gaze was fixed on the horizon, and there, like a monstrous vision, she saw Prince Stanislaus on horseback, a smoking pistol in his hand, grinning as he turned his horse and galloped away.

There was more noise behind her, shouting, footsteps running from the inn. In a nightmare she turned and saw the landlord reach the Marquis just as he fell to the ground, an ugly red stain spreading across his chest.

# CHAPTER TEN

For the rest of her life Lavina never forgot the next few terrible hours.

For years her dreams were haunted by the memory of running up to the Marquis as he lay bleeding on the ground, throwing herself onto him with a cry of, "Ivan. Oh my love, my love! You must not be dead. You cannot be. Don't leave me!"

She put her arms about him and held him to her, sobbing.

Then some men came running, fetched by the landlord, lifted him and carried him inside to a bedroom.

The landlord was a kind, sensible man. He dispatched a messenger for the doctor, and another to the McEwuans.

Luckily the doctor was close by and arrived quickly. He extracted the bullet, and managed to stop the bleeding.

"It isn't as bad as it looks," he said at last. "The bullet did not strike any vital organ. With reasonable luck, he should pull through."

Lord Ringwood entered as he said these words, and took hold of his daughter to stop her from fainting with relief.

"Bear up, my darling," he said. "All will be well."

"I love him, Papa."

"I know, my dear," he said gently. "I've always

141

known."

"I didn't know myself."

He patted her hand.

"But I did."

"Can he be moved?" Sir Ian asked the doctor.

He had been at home when the message arrived, and had hurried to the inn with Lord Ringwood.

"Since your home is so close," the doctor replied, "I think you can move him that short distance."

Another message was sent to fetch the McEwuans' most comfortable carriage. When Lord Ringwood had thanked the landlord and paid him liberally, they began the short journey back to the McEwuan castle.

Lavina sat beside the Marquis, holding his hand between both hers. But he sat with his eyes closed with an expression of pain on his white face. And she could not tell if he were aware of her or not.

It was a relief to see him carried away to his room, and to know that he would be more comfortable.

Propriety forbade her to follow while he was being undressed, so she stayed with her father, and told him everything that had happened. He was shocked, and when she was finally able to return to the Marquis she left the Earl sunk in deep thought.

The Marquis had briefly regained consciousness in the inn, but now he sank back. The journey had disturbed him, bringing on a fever. The doctor administered laudanum, which calmed him slightly, but Lavina watched in horror as his eyes grew sunken and his face assumed a deathly pallor.

As his fever mounted he began to mutter deliriously. She strained to hear the words, but could only make out a few, and they did not make any sense.

"A spinning top – " he repeated again and again, "pretty as a spinning top – "

For one long, interminable night he repeated these words. Sometimes he would open his eyes and look straight at Lavina, but without any recognition, before closing them again.

Then, nearing morning, he fell into a troubled sleep. Mercifully his temperature had fallen, but he seemed distant from her, like a man living in another world.

"If only I knew some way to reach him," she murmured desperately.

Then suddenly she had an idea.

She went quickly out of the room and down the stairs, to find Lady McEwuan.

"I have come to ask you a great favour," she said.

"My dear, anything."

"Is there a piano anywhere upstairs?"

Lady McEwuan stared at her.

"A piano!" she exclaimed.

She was about to ask questions. Then she changed her mind and said:

"There is one in the nursery which the children used until they grew older. I've kept it tuned."

"Oh thank you, that will be wonderful. May I have it moved?"

"Of course. Tell the butler what you want, and he will send someone."

On Lavina's instruction the butler had two men carry the piano from the nursery into the passage outside the room where the Marquis was sleeping.

She crept back into his room. His eyes were half closed and she could not tell if he was awake or sleeping. She slipped out again, leaving the door open.

In the corridor Lavina sat down at the piano. Then she started to play the soft music she had first heard the Marquis play when they were on the yacht.

She played the tune which the Marquis himself had played so well, and which she knew meant a great deal to him.

She played for twenty minutes. Then, very softly, she looked back into the bedroom.

He lay quite still, his eyes completely closed now, his breathing coming more easily. Whether he was asleep or merely listening, she had no idea.

For a moment she stood where she was, thinking that he looked somehow at peace and not suffering from pain or fever.

She returned to the piano and began to play again, some of her own favourite tunes.

Then once more she played the tune which meant so much to the man she loved.

Only after quite a long time had passed did she once again look into the room, and tip-toe nearer to the bed.

His eyes opened and he said very quietly, in a voice she could hardly hear,

"Thank you, my darling."

For a moment Lavina was so astonished that she could only stare down at the Marquis and could not speak.

Then as he put out his hand very slowly towards her, she slipped hers into it.

"Do you feel better?" she asked. "Are you in terrible pain?"

She felt his fingers close over hers and he said,

"I feel no pain now, for I have been listening to the things you told me through the music."

"What – did you hear me tell you?" she asked.

"You said you were sorry for me, and also that I mean something to you."

"Everyone is very worried about you," Lavina

managed to say. "I can only tell you of my feelings by playing on the piano that which I cannot say in words."

"And as I listened to you, I began to feel better," the Marquis said.

He was speaking in a low voice, almost hesitating between the words. But Lavina could hear every one of them, because she was listening with her heart.

Her hand was still in his. She felt somehow as if she were giving him the strength he had lost.

"I have been so frightened for you," she whispered.

"When I heard the music, I felt that you were giving me help and strength, and I should soon be well."

"Oh yes," Lavina answered softly. "You must get well. Life is so sad without you."

"I want you here, I want you to help me," the Marquis said. "Please play for me again. Then I will feel strong enough to tell you what I want to say."

"Tell me now," she begged, breathless with hope.

But his eyes were already closed.

She took her hand from his, but she had the strange feeling that he released her reluctantly.

She went into the corridor, and once again played the tunes which she loved herself, and which she felt expressed in music what she felt when she was riding, dancing or just looking at the sun.

She knew now that her music spoke to the man she loved, and that the things it told him were vital for them both, and the future.

"You must get well, completely well," she told him in music. "I love you more than I can ever say, except in this music which seems to come down from heaven and not belong to the world."

After a while she thought she would see if he was asleep or awake. She went into the room very quietly and found his eyes closed.

She knelt beside him, praying that he would soon get well, closing her own eyes as she did so. When she opened them she saw him looking at her.

As she looked back at him he put out his hand. She put hers into his and felt him hold her hand so firmly that he was almost squeezing it.

Then he asked quietly,

"Were you praying for me?"

"With all my heart," she replied fervently. "You must get well, for my sake."

"Does it matter to you," he murmured, "if I am well or not?"

"Of course it does," she said passionately.

"I thought you hated me."

"No, no I could never hate you."

"Promise me that that is true."

"It is true, I swear it."

She would have said more but he seemed to fall asleep again, and this time it was as though something had brought him peace.

Her father had crept into the room behind her.

"Go and get some sleep now, my dear," he said. "He'll be better in the morning."

That night she slept without dreaming, and woke feeling calmer.

"He's better," said Mrs Banty, without waiting for her first question. "I've already been along to find out."

Mrs Banty had developed a soft spot for the Marquis.

"I must go to him," Lavina said.

"When you've had some breakfast," Mrs Banty said firmly.

She went downstairs to be greeted warmly by the

146

whole McEwuan family. Suddenly she was hungry. She had eaten so little recently, and her spirits were rising with hope.

Suddenly the butler entered, his face grave, for he understood the significance of what he was saying.

"The Queen's messenger is here to see Lord Ringwood."

"Papa!" Lavina's hands flew to her mouth.

"It's all right, my dear. It will be a reply to the letter I despatched to Her Majesty as soon as I knew what Prince Stanislaus had done."

"But what did you say to her?"

"I resigned my place at court, and I told her why."

Before she could reply the messenger appeared. It was Sir Richard Peyton again, and his manner could only be described as chastened.

"The Queen has received your letter," he said, "and replied at once. I have travelled all night to be here, and I am commanded by Her Majesty to say that she hopes you will take the contents of her letter very seriously."

Under the anxious eyes of everyone, Lord Ringwood opened the envelope.

It contained Her Majesty's urgent plea that Lord Ringwood would reconsider his decision to leave the court, as she could not do without him.

Her Majesty further added her congratulations on the betrothal of Lady Lavina Ringwood to Lord Elswick, and her hopes of happiness for their future.

She thought Lord Ringwood might be interested to known that Prince Stanislaus had left the country and would not be returning.

"We have won, my dear," he said to Lavina, tears of joy in his eyes.

"Oh Papa!"

She hugged her father, full of relief, for him as much

as herself.

"Will you return to court?" she asked.

"I think so, my dear."

"I must go and tell him," she said, and sped upstairs.

She found the Marquis lying quietly, but looking much better than yesterday. There was colour in his cheeks.

"We have won," she said, and told him about the letter.

"Yes," he said, "but I am still wondering exactly what I have won – or whether I have won anything. You will have to tell me."

"Don't you know?" she asked, sitting by his bed. "Didn't the music tell you?"

"It gave me hope. But you were so very angry with me? Has your anger truly died?"

"I was foolish to say those things when we were at the inn. I was distraught. It was just such a shock to hear Stanislaus tell me why you wanted revenge on him. Of course, I always realized that there was something that I didn't know.

"When Papa and I came to see you, you refused us at first, then changed your mind, and later I remembered that it was when Stanislaus was mentioned. And you always told me that you had your own reasons."

"Yes, I wanted revenge on him for what he'd done to me," the Marquis said. "But not only for my own sake. I was revenging her as well."

"Her? You mean – "

"Anjelica, the girl I once loved. I can see the truth about her now. She was a greedy little predator, who wanted me because I was heir to wealth and a great title.

"For her sake, I became an outcast from my family, but that wasn't what she wanted. It would have meant waiting, perhaps years, for me to inherit, and she wanted the good things of life immediately.

148

"Stanislaus tempted her away with gold and finery. He couldn't marry her, but she didn't care for that, as long as there was luxury. But it lasted only a few months before he threw her out."

"Yes, he told me," Lavina said. "He almost boasted of it."

"She sank into poverty and lived such a wretched life that she finally lost her wits. That was how she was when I found her again."

"You found her?" Lavina asked, startled.

"Yes, quite by chance. She was very frail by then, and didn't know me. I was able to take her away and put her in the care of kindly people, who looked after her until she died."

"You did that for her?" Lavina asked in wonder. "After what she had done to you?"

"It wasn't entirely her fault. She wasn't really very intelligent, and she fell easy prey to his pretty lies. So I felt I had her to avenge as well as myself."

"And society called you a curmudgeon, who hated women," she said in wonder.

He gave her a crooked smile.

"Society was right, except that it wasn't only women I hated, but the whole world, that could exact such a brutal price. I condemned all women as faithless and stupid, and all men as boorish and cruel. I shut myself up with my misery and bitterness, allowing no good healthy light to fall on it.

"In all those years I can recall only one thing that brought me joy. And that was the night I walked into a house in London and saw a young girl dancing like a ray of sunlight."

He smiled tenderly.

"I can see her now, a spinning top, her dark hair flying out as she whirled. She was like the embodiment of life

149

itself, young, beautiful, unafraid."

"I thought you despised me," she said.

"I turned away from you because you threatened the iron prison in which I had enclosed myself. I told myself you were only a child – which was true, but not my real reason. The real reason was that I rejected the gifts of life and joy that you carried with you. I was afraid of them.

"But I never forgot you. In the years since, your spinning figure has haunted my dreams and danced across my vision, never allowing me to forget that I had chosen a terrible path; that there was another path, if only I dared take it.

"And then, one day, you returned, grown up, glorious, majestic, asking my help.

"But by that time I was in no state to appreciate you. If you hadn't come into my life when you did, it would soon have been all up with me.

"And yet you seemed to resent me, and be angry with me.

"I fought you. You'll never know how hard I fought you. I didn't want the warmth and life you brought with you. I'd lived so long away from them that they were too much for me.

"And yet, while I fought you with one hand I tightened my grip on you with the other. I put bolts and bars on our engagement, anything to keep you with me – and all the time I told myself that it was revenge on Stanislaus that motivated me. Nothing else. But the truth was I was daily falling more and more in love with you.

"I didn't want to admit it to myself, but in my heart I knew. And then, when I thought I was going to die, I knew I had to speak to you, to tell you that I loved you, and wanted your love."

His eyes held hers. She felt they were saying

something to her she did not understand, something more than his lips spoke.

Then he said very quietly,

"I love you. I have loved you for a long time. I am only afraid that I might lose you."

The words seemed to come slowly from his lips.

But his hand tightened and somehow she found herself bending nearer to him until his lips touched hers.

She loved him as she had never loved anyone before.

"I love you! I love you!" he said.

Then once again his lips were holding hers captive.

She thought it was the most wonderful and the most glorious thing she had ever known.

"I love you! I love you!" she wanted to say, but it was impossible to speak when the Marquis's lips were against hers.

Both his arms went round her to hold her closer still.

It seemed a long time later that Lavina found herself lying on the bed beside him. Her head was on his shoulder.

"Tell me that you love me," he begged.

"I love you!" Lavina whispered. "It is so wonderful that I can't find words to express it."

"All I want," the Marquis said, "are your lips. Kiss me again and I will know I am not dreaming and that this is real."

She kissed him again, gently and tenderly, so as not to disturb his wound.

"How soon can we be married?" he asked.

"Do you really want to marry me?" Lavina asked.

"I am going to make certain that you belong to me, and I never lose you," he said. "You are mine and you must swear to me, on everything you hold sacred, you will never leave me."

"I promise I will never do that," Lavina replied. "I

think I first loved you when I heard you playing the piano, and the music seemed to whisper of the love which I had never known, and never felt until I met you."

"I always knew that you were different from any woman I had met before," he mused, "but I was desperately afraid of frightening you, and making you and your father have no further use for me once we reached Scotland."

"Even when I thought I was annoyed with you, you were in my heart. You were so different from any other man I had ever met."

"And every man you will meet in the future," he said softly. "You are my darling, and I will never let you look at another man."

"I'll never want to do that. I want to be with you, to be close to you and for you to love me, just as the music told me about love. That is how I feel at the moment."

"I have a great deal more than music to tell you about," the Marquis said. "You are everything I ever wanted and ever longed for in a woman. I swear to you, my darling, I will do everything to make you happy!"

"And I will make you happy," she promised him, "so that you will forget the years of sadness. There are so many wonderful things we can do together."

"I love you, from the top of your head to the soles of your feet," he said. "I shall love you until the time comes for my life to end."

"On that day," Lavina said, "my life too will be over. I want nothing in the world but you."

She was unable to say any more because the Marquis's lips were on hers. She felt as he kissed her as if they were both flying up into the sky to be blessed by God.

She knew, in her mind and in her heart, that she had found love. And that she would be true to that love forever more.